I0692782

DRAGON'S HEART

RED PLANET DRAGONS OF TAJSS BOOK TEN

MIRANDA MARTIN

CONTENTS

KATE

I carefully cut a slit along the side of the lychnara's thick, yellow peel, not wanting to lose any of the sweet juice inside. The rare fruit is a much-appreciated treat, one we would most likely never have found if Gomul wasn't nice enough to procure them for us. We have a lot to thank him for.

I set my blade down and peel the fruit just as slowly, purposefully focused on the task. Maybe I don't need to be so careful about it—scratch that, I know I don't need to be so careful about it—but the task gives me something less irritating to pay attention to.

"We need to stay here. It doesn't make any sense to leave the safety of this place."

I pull out a segment of the fruit and pop it into my mouth. The juicy sweetness bursts across my tongue. It's at the perfect ripeness. I think of my response as I chew thoughtfully. I don't want to step on Annabel's toes. But it's getting more and more difficult to simply go along with her plans when I don't fully agree with them—or agree with them at all lately. Her delivery also leaves much to be desired, to be honest.

"I think it's a little premature to decide on a permanent home when we've explored so little of this place," I finally venture in a mild tone. "Maybe there's something more suited to us out there."

Annabel scowls at me, her pretty features obscured by the expression.

"That's ridiculous," she snaps, brushing her long blonde hair behind her shoulder. I wonder if she spends time every night brushing it for a thousand strokes. She's the type to do something so frivolous. "We know it's safe here. Thanks to Gomul, we have food and shelter. Don't you remember how terrible it is out there? How hot, how desolate? It would be foolhardy to leave something like this behind." She shakes her head, glancing at the others. "No—we need to stay here, where the elder Zmaj has managed to keep us alive while we learn to fend for ourselves."

I shove another piece of fruit in my mouth to keep quiet.

I fully appreciate Gomul's kindness. When he found us, we were trying to escape pursuit from one of the crazy-dangerous animals on this planet.

The giant, hump-backed lizard thing with the razor-sharp teeth that Gomul called a guster could have easily killed all of us. Our ability to defend ourselves here is a joke. The sight of the Zmaj with his massive body, wings, and tail, his weapon slashing through the air, only underscored that fact.

He didn't have to take us in, provide shelter for us in his network of underground tunnels. He didn't have to donate one of the tunnels to us, give us a home when we really needed it. I can appreciate all that, appreciate the relative safety we've found here, but I don't know if that means we should keep building in this tunnel. Should we keep using all our time and energy to make this a permanent home?

Yes, it's reinforced and secure, a relic of an old civilization that obviously knew what they were doing. However, there's so much more to this planet, so much more we haven't even bothered to explore yet! Settling down here without even trying to see what else there is seems remarkably short-sighted to me.

Also, how are we still learning to fend for ourselves here? We've been here for years! If we don't know how to be self-sufficient yet, we're never going to learn. At least not here, where our basic needs are already taken care of.

I keep my head down as I swallow the food in my mouth. I don't know how everyone else feels. Are they battling the same volatile mix of emotions that keep rising in me?

Despite what Annabel thinks or says, I know that if I stay without at least trying to get out there, something inside me, something vital, will start to wither, especially under Annabel's leadership. She can be overbearing, stubborn in her views, seemingly uncaring of what everyone else really thinks as long as she gets her way. Being loud isn't a way to win an argument, not really, but I feel like Annabel is relying on that cheap tactic more and more the longer we're holed up here.

Even if this is the best place for us, we shouldn't settle here. At least, not yet.

I refuse to believe we're the sole survivors. We can't be the only ones. I know we're not. Not with that many people on board the ship! There are other survivors here on Tajss—I can feel that truth in my very bones.

If I'm right, our shipmates could be out there enduring the very worst this place has to offer while we sit here in relative comfort. The glaring sun, the heat, the dangerous predators, and even just the sheer difficulty of finding the basics of food and water. Never mind the fact that some of them were bound to be injured if they survived. Although Gomul has turned out to be our very own guardian angel, there's no guarantee that the others of his kind are cut from the same altruistic cloth. They could be antagonistic, even violent. Who knows?

All of that runs through my head while Annabel speaks. I can see now isn't the time to broach the subject. She already has that stubborn look on her face, the one that says nothing will change her mind right now. She'll only dig into her stance deeper if I say anything.

"Now, if we can just be efficient with this renovation, we can all be more comfortable," Annabel continues. "That means being careful and not wasting time tinkering with the tools," she adds, pointedly looking at Nora. "A little less air-headedness would be greatly appreciated."

Nora immediately looks down, hunching her shoulders and allowing her bangs to fall over her face. She often uses the curtain of her straight brown hair to hide if she doesn't want to engage.

Irritation rises in me as I see the gentle woman withdraw. I'm really starting to hate the little demeaning comments Annabel likes to make.

Nora isn't hurting anything. She just likes to tinker with things, likes to count them and study them. She was a lab clerk on the ship with a limited expertise in botany and pharmaceuticals. I don't know if keeping inventory was ingrained in her on the job or if the job was right for her because she has a slight obsession with it. In any case, it doesn't hurt anybody.

We need all the little joys we can get in this place to keep what sanity we can. The sight of her reaction to the comment is enough to throw me over the edge. I've used up all my restraint by this time. I know I shouldn't say anything, but—

"Nora is a dreamer," Nina inserts in her placating voice, attempting to soften Annabel's insult. Always the peacemaker, Nina is Annabel's PR pet. She uses that same soothing voice she once used to put clients at ease in the independently owned spa on the ship. Now she's constantly trying to smooth out that cutting edge to Annabel's increasingly tyrannical tone in "leadership."

I understand her need to keep the peace, to keep tension down. We need each other here. If we're always fighting, it will just make things harder for everyone. But when it comes to Annabel, I feel like her efforts are akin to slapping a Band-Aid on a gunshot wound. What's the point?

However, just like many times in the past, the addition of her comment does succeed in derailing the comment I was going to make, so maybe it's more effective than I think. Annabel sure is keeping the woman on her toes. Smoothing things over after her sharp comments is basically a full-time job.

Every time Our Glorious Leader feels challenged or her mood dips for who-knows-what reason, real or perceived, Annabel starts shooting out insults, as if putting everyone else down will improve her own mood. She's a bully, plain and simple. She doesn't even really appreciate Nina's attempts to keep the fights to a minimum. Like now.

Rolling her eyes, Annabel throws down the biscuit made from the underground rice Gomul harvests several times a year. Standing, she looks over her shoulder at me as she heads towards the dens.

"Clear the meal circle, Kate," she tosses out, the command curt and dismissive. Designed to be insulting. She really doesn't like it that I didn't agree with her.

I don't take the bait, even as I feel my cheeks flush with

anger and embarrassment. Everyone else around me is silent in sympathy, which only makes things worse. I finish my meal quietly, then stand and leave, not looking at anyone when I do. I'm not following that order. Not this time.

Annabel's diva act is getting old.

I know my small rebellion isn't going to be without consequences, but I've had enough for tonight. I'd rather take the repercussions than follow along like a good little girl.

The next day, it doesn't take long for the fallout to rear its head. Annabel makes me pay for not falling in line with task after menial task.

"Go gather the herbs we need for dinner," she demands, that knowing glint in her eye. She's almost goading me into saying something, but I'm not going to give her the satisfaction.

So I go to the areas in the safe spaces of the tunnel system where the herbs grow. The walls shimmer, reflecting the light of the torch. Moisture, probably the most precious resource there is on Tajss. As I go deeper into the caverns the spot between my shoulders itches the entire time. The small movements I make echo in the dim rooms. It's safe; I know that. But that doesn't mean I don't feel creeped out going into the spaces farther away from the area where we mainly live down here.

It's fine. It's all in my hea—

My heart jerks in my chest as something loud bangs nearby. Looking around, eyes wide, straining to see past the flickering flames of the torch in my hand, it takes everything in me not to run back. I scan every shadow, each motion an undefined threat. Barely daring to breathe, my heartbeat loud in my ears, I strain for any hint of what caused the sound, skin crawling as I know I'm about to die.

Nothing happens. My heart slows and the hair on the back of my neck lies down. I've got enough herbs, Annabel can deal with it. Walking backwards up the tunnel, I turn around at last and manage to keep myself to a brisk walk instead of a flat out run. I'll take my wins where I can get them.

When I make it back, I'm greeted with another unpleasant task.

Joy.

"Kate, you're going to have to wash another load of clothing."

Annabel's lips turn up slightly at the corners when she gives me that order, her eyes watching me expectantly. She's enjoying this.

I've already done my share of the clothes and she knows that. I want to tell her to shove them up her ass, but I grit my teeth and just do it. This won't kill me. It's just annoying. Like most of the things she does.

Interspersed with those tasks, she also adds multiple message runs to Gomul, ones that are clearly unnecessary, not at all urgent like she claims they are. Does she think I'm an errand girl?

My temper is building with each additional order she gives me, despite my intention to let everything flow off my back. I'm going to say something else she isn't going to like. I know I am. It's only a matter of time before I break under the mountain of tiny slights.

How does she think this is going to end? With me apologizing and kissing her ring?

I sigh as I make the trip to Gomul again. At least it gets me away from her pettiness for a while. That's something.

I turn the corner to Gomul's section of the tunnels, the metal framework just like ours, but the interior improved. He's had much more time to make his area a home. His bedroom is walled off, a kitchen and sitting area neatly organized just outside it. I've never seen things out of place. I wish I was as organized as he is.

When I arrive this time, there's a pot of something fragrant boiling over the fire, and he isn't surprised to see me show up with yet another message.

"Yes?" he asks mildly, stirring the hot liquid with a ladle.

"Annabel wanted me to let you know there are beasts circling outside."

I feel more than a little ridiculous relaying that particular message when he's survived here for who knows how long, completely by himself. I'm sure he's well aware of any dangers nearby. More aware than any of us likely are. When he smiles at me gently without acknowledging the message, I wince a little inside.

"Would you like to sit and enjoy a hot beverage with me?" he asks, gesturing to one of the stools he has set up around the fire.

I take a deep breath and let it out, my shoulders relaxing.

"That sounds wonderful," I say sincerely. I could use a breather. I've taken just about all I can take and I'm close to the breaking point.

Gomul nods, going over to a shelf and bringing back two cups.

He ladles some of the hot liquid from the pot into one of the cups and hands it over to me.

"Thank you," I say, taking it from him, cupping it with both hands. A sweet aroma wafts from it which I inhale deeply.

He nods graciously, filling his own cup. The firelight is kind to his lightly lined face, the silver streaks in his hair. He's older, though I don't know exactly how old, and I don't want to pry. The light also highlights his pretty scales, the iridescent surfaces eye-catching.

I take a sip of the drink. It's a gentle tea, one that feels soothing on the throat. Tension drains out of my shoulders and I take a deep breath, letting it out slowly. I didn't realize exactly how much I needed a break until right then. Keeping my guard up and fighting against my own emotions has taken its toll.

Gomul takes a seat across from me, taking a sip from his own cup. A moment of comfortable silence descends as we sit there with our tea. I'm staring at the flickering flames, my mind drifting, so I start a little when Gomul breaks the quiet. I don't expect him to break it the way he does.

"There are times when people find themselves in roles that feel uncomfortable." He looks up from his cup, meeting my eyes. "Often, the reason is that they are not suited to the role. Do not naturally fit into the parameters of it."

I frown. What is he trying to say?

"The group needs to work together," I finally say vaguely, not knowing how else to respond.

He must be speaking of my role, but he isn't being direct about it.

"Yes," he agrees. "Unity is often required for survival here on Tajss." He leans forward towards me, his gaze intent. "However, a spear is only good if the tip is sharp. Without a good leader, a group cannot be strong. Even if united."

Who he is speaking of now is quite clear.

"Annabel is trying her best," I venture, though the words sound hollow even to me.

Gomul sits back up, his shrug saying more than such a simple gesture should be able to.

"Perhaps. And if that is the case...then perhaps a new point is required." He tilts his head to the side, considering me. "Perhaps a part of the whole that does not quite fit in the role she is currently playing."

I narrow my eyes at him. His point is thinly veiled. Heck, there may as well be no veil.

"What are you trying to say?" I demand.

His smile widens, humor twinkling in his eyes.

"Strength often recognizes strength. And clashes with it. It is the nature of many creatures to fight for dominance." He raises a brow at me. "Isn't it interesting that Annabel so often finds herself at odds with one person in particular?"

I break the eye contact, not able to maintain it with that knowing gaze. It's too piercing. Too insightful. Too painful. Because he's right. The realization has been brewing at the back of my mind for a long time now, despite my efforts to push it away. That is a level of responsibility that feels over-whelming, scary. Maybe I've been suppressing it for too long. I've been ignoring what my gut has been trying to tell me when I should have been listening to it instead.

Gomul's right. Annabel isn't right to lead us, judging only by the direction she's taken us. We need to leave and find the others. If she refuses to see that...

Maybe Annabel shouldn't be in charge.

2

ERROL

I place the triangular piece of meteorite glass between two others, then press down the smooth edges to ensure it is secure. I catch myself holding my breath, as if breathing could break the glass. The starburst patterns I've been slowly working into the nearly finished wall take some time to design and a good amount of concentration to execute properly, but I do not mind. In fact, I enjoy it.

Adding the ornate decoration is soothing, in a way. I can lose myself in selecting just the right piece of the shimmering glass to harmonize well with the pieces around it. My focus sinks into the patterns and shapes and I think only about the visual appeal of it all. It does not leave much room to worry or dwell on things that do not yield productive results.

Stepping back to survey what I have accomplished so far, I'm surprised to see that it is quite a bit. When I am working so close to the design, it is difficult to picture the whole. The light from the suns plays over the ripple of glass. The lovely dance of the rays catches the eye and holds the attention. Just as I had hoped. Not only can it be spotted from afar, acting as a beacon to guide us home, I also hope it will brighten everyone's spirits.

Casting another critical eye over my progress, I nod to myself. It looks straight and even, but not too perfect because the glass shards are not regularly sized or shaped. I like that it is not too uniform. The appearance is pretty and accessible rather than perfect and untouchable.

I pick up a large piece of the meteorite glass that we have all been gathering, and I hold it so the two suns' light streams through it. Wavy ripples of strong sunlight appear on the sand below. Setting the piece into place, I think about how something so beautiful could come from something so destructive.

It is almost a metaphor for life itself, really. Even the most terrible events could yield something unexpectedly beautiful in the end. I like that idea. It is a thought that I hold onto in day-to-day life. After all, hope is a fragile thing. It must be protected and fostered to survive, so I must do my part. In terms of our community, the meteorite glass is one of my contributions towards improving our home.

Recently, there has been an increased focus on making life in in our new caves more comfortable, with little luxuries to add enjoyment to the hard life on Tajss. I like to see that effort. I like the optimism about the future that it suggests. It has been some time since I have felt that soft emotion. I want it to stay, want it to linger and grow.

It quiets the ghosts of the past that haunt me. I would rather forget them entirely. I wonder if any of the others feel the cold touch of those memories during their weaker moments.

I step back and slide the back of my hand over my forehead to wipe away the sweat, straightening to ease the ache in the small of my back from bending over for a long time.

Just as I do, Penelope appears next to me with water. She is a welcome sight.

"How was your trip?" I ask, taking the water gratefully. "Thank you."

Her eyes twinkle and her cheeks flush at the question.

Ah.

Bashir must have ensured that lovers' trip was splendid indeed. I can see the glow in her that was missing before she let Bashir come closer. I am glad that it is there now. She was always a bright female, but she was lonely—and largely unaware of that fact. I may have been the only one who noticed that dullness in her, that lack of shine that indicated she was not entirely happy.

I was paying attention because I have yet to lay eyes on my own true mate.

It leaves me constantly searching the females around me, looking for that spark that joins lovers. That spark that I so desire. Unfortunately, though there are plenty of beauties, there are none whom I look at and feel the cry in my soul, *you! you belong to me.* I have been searching for so long that in my most bleak moments, I begin to wonder if there is even a mate for me at all among the shipwrecked. That burst of hope I felt at our first contact with the humans has faded greatly in the years since.

But Penelope does not know that. She simply smiles brightly at my question.

"It was wonderful," she says sincerely, stepping back with the now-empty water vessel. Her eye wanders over to the wall itself and brightens even more. "Your work is looking gorgeous, Errol. The wall looks a whole lot less like a prison enclosure."

I smile back at her, chuckling, trying not to reveal the ache in my own heart at not having that connection to another that she has found.

"My thanks," I murmur.

She nods, still smiling as she turns around to continue passing out water from more vessels to the others still building the structure of the wall. It nearly spans the entire entrance to the valley now, erected to prevent any dangerous threats from making it in too close to our home caves.

I sigh, turning back to the glass. It is no matter. Life is much better than it has been for decades. Even if I do not have a mate.

Pushing the thought aside firmly, I focus on the wall again, sink back into that mindset that allows the unpleasant thoughts and emotions to drift away.

I settle back into my rhythm, the smooth glass slipping through my fingertips. Creating something beautiful. I am so absorbed in the work that I do not break until the grumbling in my stomach calls the time to my attention. It's past dinner already.

Gazing over the work I've done, a sense of satisfaction swells. It's good. The design itself, in a way, is one of hope. All these years past, resigned to our fate, none of us created art. We were going through the motions of life without actually living. The human arrival changed everything.

Walking out of the cave, Tajss' two suns sit on the horizon, casting long shadows over the rolling sand dunes, creating the unique beauty that is my home. The striated colors of the dunes, shades of red to white, shift with the winds. It's beautiful and breathtaking. I find it joyful that I notice it again.

My protective lenses close making it easy to stare out to the setting suns. Inhaling the crisp, dry air I let it out in a slow exhale. This is good. Everything is better.

"Let it be," Padraig yells in his deep bass voice.

Glancing to where he's working with the others on the protective wall, which is almost done, Padraig stands with his massive arms crossed glaring. That's not surprising since he's always glowering at someone.

"I'm almost done," Samil calls down from the top of the wall.

"It's dinner," Padraig barks.

Samil has grown bolder, which is good, he's standing up to Padraig. Ignoring the two males, I inspect the wall from here. It's solid, well built, and should be enough to keep the wandering animals out of our area. Padraig's gate made of metal salvaged from the human's wrecked ship is an excellent addition.

Turning from the wall towards the common cave, the females' garden is in full bloom. It's stunning to see so much color growing in one place. Almost as if they've created their own oasis, which in a way they have.

Tall stalks shift as something causes them to move. My scales itch as I rush over, suspecting some creature has invaded. Pushing the stalks to one side, sparkling blue eyes stare up at me and Zoe points, laughing.

"Zoe!" I exclaim, crouching down in front of her.

She's a beautiful baby. Her perfect scales reflect the setting suns in glinting rainbows. Her cheeks, always full, seem to be fuller than normal and she doesn't answer with words, only smiles. Shaking my head, I tsk at her.

"Zoe?" I ask, tilting my head. She nods her head acknowledging that's her name. "Open your mouth."

She shakes her head side to side then swallows with great difficulty. Only then does she open her mouth.

"Me good," she says, her soft voice music to my ears.

"You know your mother doesn't want you eating before dinner," I admonish.

She looks sheepishly around then grins. "Okay," she says, shrugging, obviously undeterred.

"Come, let's eat," I say, holding out my hand and extending a finger.

She takes my finger in her tiny hand and we walk together to the communal meal table. Her tiny tail swishes behind her as she bounds step to step, determined to keep up with my much longer stride.

"Trouble, Err-yll?" she asks, glancing up.

"No, Zoe, I won't say anything," I smile. "But you eat your dinner, okay?"

"Yes!" she exclaims, dropping my finger and running ahead.

Olivia sees her running and intercepts, scooping her up into her arms and kissing her on both cheeks. Zoe giggles loudly and everyone, no matter what they're doing, stops to watch for a moment.

Hope. Such a beautiful thing.

Grabbing a plate, I fill it then take a seat at the table with the others.

"Come on!" Arawn says.

"That was not fair!" Bashir responds.

I laugh along with the others as I take another bite of the meat dish drenched with Delilah's special sauce and watch the checkers match. Right now, Bashir and Arawn are playing against each other. Everyone else crowds around while we eat. We have come to truly enjoy the games our new additions brought along with them. They engage our minds with something a little more frivolous than our normal day-to-day activities, and bring out our competitive spirits in a safe manner.

I take another bite of the food, savoring the flavors as they burst across my tongue. Delilah's special sauce really is second to none. Like the others, I am grateful she has found a way to replicate her old recipe here. Though I am also sad for her at the same time.

The humans must make their home on Tajss now. There is no choice, not with their ship, their only means of transportation off the planet, completely destroyed. I sense that reality is not an easy one for the humans to stomach. It wouldn't be for anyone.

Tajss is a hard place to live, but I cannot imagine living elsewhere. This is home, all I've ever known. It wasn't always this bad, before the Devastation, Tajss was a thriving planet. The only source of epis for the galaxy, it was an important place. Still dangerous, yes, but bustling with life.

I can sense the restlessness in the females' spirits over having to accept life here. I understand it. This is not their home. This was not the future they imagined for themselves.

Even their bodies are not meant to be in such a harsh climate, let alone their minds. They are soft, not created for a place with predators who can so easily overwhelm them. Their tender skin can be easily burned by our suns or scratched by the sand that Tajss is made of.

That is why the little things are so important. Partaking in comforts like the sauce that reminds them of their past and these games that engage our minds—it eases my spirit because I know it brings the humans joy.

I want them to be happy here. And these small things do help. I know because they also help me, help subdue my natural inclination for worry, quiet the memories of my past that plague me.

It is as if all of us agree we need to have more play, more frivolity in our lives, so we continue with the games even after dinner is over, playfully calling out insults and teasing the losers. I smile to myself, content with the happy, relaxed mood. This is a life worth working hard for, so much better than the quiet melancholy, waiting for our race to end.

Unfortunately, that mood does not last.

A harsh grinding sound quiets everyone and we all listen

in the silence. I immediately reach for my lochaber as soon as I hear it. It came from the wall. I and the other males run out and swiftly down the valley, worried what we will find. My heart picks up speed as I see the top of the wall lurch, a small amount of dust falling from it.

I take a step towards it just as the creature behind the wall rears its head. The short muzzle, the leathery gray skin, the mane of thick white hair just under its massive head...

Chatteron. It is a chatteron. Well outside its natural habitat. Bashir had mentioned seeing one and killing it at the New Village, another area a chatteron should not have been. It is huge, walking on all fours, its feet a mixture of paws and a birdlike foot with long sharp claws. If we do not stop it now, it could damage the incomplete wall. Almost before the thought even forms, I am sprinting towards the creature.

My heart pounds, pumping adrenaline through me. Tightening my grip on my lochaber, I glance at the others running beside me. The bijass rises, pushing itself into my thoughts, a primal need to fight.

The ground trembles beneath my feet as it hits the wall again, roaring as it opens its mouth to reveal razor-sharp teeth, it's deep red tongue slim and pointed as it flicks out to taste the air.

The wall cannot take much more. It is battering a newer section, one not set quite as firmly as the sections that have had more time to cure.

Flaring my wings, I leap into the air, my lochaber pulled back, the grip I have on the shaft tight. Slashing downwards with the blade, I touch down briefly on its broad back and leap onto the ground behind it. It is bad luck that I missed the eyes, but a cut opens just above them.

The creature roars, its head turning towards me. I barely dodge its teeth as it lunges at me, slashing with my lochaber at its softer underbelly.

Behind it, I see the shadows of my fellow Zmaj leaping over the wall, but I cannot stop and watch. I roll between the thing's legs to avoid its whipping tail, just as Padraig stabs at the vulnerable area below its jaw. Melchior follows up with another slash at its underbelly.

Distracted by the others and attempting to blink away the blood flowing freely from my cut above its eyes, the chatteron does not see Bashir as he launches off the wall and onto its back. He slashes just under the thing's jaw, before the protective mane.

The creature tries to buck Bashir off, and I take my opportunity at the distraction. Stabbing upwards from underneath, I bury my lochaber into its body, shoving with so much force that I bury it almost halfway up the handle.

I feel the tip cut into its heart.

This time, the roar it emits is more of a gurgle. It is bleeding both outside and in. There is no recovering from a heart blow. With a hard jerk to pull out my weapon, I roll out from underneath it.

Bashir leaps off its back, the others also moving back to a safe distance as the creature falters. It is in its death throes. It stumbles towards us, but it is bleeding much too badly, its heart too wounded for it to survive for more than a few steps. With a whistling whine, it finally stops. It slowly lists to the side before it finally succumbs and hits the ground.

I brace my feet and bend my knees, using my wings to stabilize myself as the ground reverberates under the full weight of the creature.

Silence as we all stare at it.

If the wall had not been there, we wouldn't have had that warning. People would likely have been hurt or worse. Some of the females have now made it to our position, their excited voices reaching me past the haze of violence.

"What the hell is that thing?"

"The wall was almost a goner!"

I look up at the wall reflexively, noticing the slight imperfections in the newly laid bricks at the top of the wall. They will survive. We can repair any minor cracks.

I look over as someone slaps me on the back.

"Good kill," Bashir praises me.

"I had help," I murmur.

He nods, looking back at the creature. "Together we are stronger."

And that is the truth is it not? We need to stay together to survive.

The talk quickly turns over from identifying the beast to what to do with the carcass itself.

"This is not meat that we should waste," Melchior points out.

I nod, murmuring my agreement along with everyone else. It is most definitely not meat to waste. It will keep us fed for a significant amount of time.

"At least there's some silver lining to this," Penelope murmurs next to me.

I have heard this phrase multiple times now. And it is very appropriate for this incident. Our course of action decided, all of us band together and start working on the carcass with our knives. Even with so many hands at work, it takes a significant amount of time to harvest all the meat.

"I've never seen anything this massive," Delilah murmurs next to me. "What is it called again?"

"Chatteron," I explain. "They should not be in this area. But it is the same creature Bashir spoke about from the New Village. The meteorite showers have likely disturbed many creatures, pushing them out of their natural homes." At least, that is what the evidence is currently pointing towards.

"I hope there aren't too many more of these nearby," she says as she continues to work. "The wall is strong, but a couple more of those things before it's finished and the mortar..."

"Yes," I agree. "The creatures are too massive for the wall to hold long if we have weak points that are still unfinished."

But the rest of the wall still looks completely intact. We did a good job of building it to withstand such force. If it is too weak to keep a creature out, what would be the point of it in the first place? Eventually, we do finish the butchering. By that point, many are exhausted and decide to go to bed for the night.

I attempt to do the same. It has been a long day with much excitement. I feel exhaustion dragging me down.

But as soon as my eyes are closed, I open them again. My thoughts are not quiet enough to drop into a slumber, no matter how much I may want to. I find myself wandering outside, not wanting to lie there when sleep will not claim me. Insomnia always brings thoughts I do not want to dwell upon.

Outside, I find Arawn is also awake, sitting in front of a checkerboard. He brightens when he sees me.

"Would you like to play?" he asks hopefully.

It is something to do, so I agree to a short game.

"The wall should be done soon," he comments after he makes his move. "I will feel much safer when it is sturdy and finished."

"Yes," I say, rubbing at my lip before I decide on my own move. "However, even though it is not yet done, it did stall the chatteron long enough that we were able to kill it before it could get to any of us."

He nods, studying the board.

"Almost as good as Delilah's sauce," he adds with a grin.

I chuckle as we move on to less serious topics. We play for some time before Arawn finally decides it is time for him to sleep. And then I am left alone.

With nothing else to distract me, I also go back to my own bed. It is later, but sleep still does not come easily, and when it finally does come, it is fitful at best and not at all restful. My dreams are vivid and confusing, a jumbled mixture of the beast's attack and of the unwanted memories I do not want to recall.

When the sun rises the next morning, I leave the bed with a sigh of relief, feeling almost more tired than when I first laid down. Not long after I am up, a messenger arrives with a fresh batch of orders from the city and a request that they arrive as quickly as possible. I let Ormarr know and he immediately starts working on fulfilling the order requests, measuring out each medicinal tonic.

Pushing back my body's call for sleep, I volunteer to be the one to travel to the city with the supplies and Ormarr accepts my offer. I do not want the wrong dreams to consume me, I do not want them penetrating my present or my future. Ever. I do not want them to be a part of my life. I intend to continue silencing my memories by staying as busy as possible.

Once Ormarr has the various mixtures of herbs steeping, I leave the room dedicated for the creation of medicines and travel towards the wall. I sink back into the meteorite glass design, keeping all my thoughts on the detailed work, but as I pick out the next perfect piece, I have another flash of the dreams from last night.

I come to a realization. What occurred last night triggered this. The felling of the beast that attempted to breach the wall and make meals of some of my people jolted these unwanted memories free. The violence and stress of the event broke through the wall I have been building inside me. Perhaps my subconscious equated that wall to the one that was almost damaged last night.

I do not know. Whatever the reason, the result is not a comfortable one.

After finishing off that section of the wall, I walk back to Ormarr's work room, trying not to think about the haunted thoughts that plague me. I need to find a way to corral these memories again. A trip across the sands should keep me sufficiently distracted.

The healer has finished packing and he hands the order over. I acknowledge that I have reached a point where I am literally running away from my past. If it helps...I'm willing.

3

KATE

I finish the fourth load of laundry I've done that day. It seems like Annabel isn't over her snit about my comment yet.

"Kate!"

I sigh, squeezing my eyes shut at Annabel's shrill call. Like I can shut it out if I don't see it happening. Maybe if I just keep walking and don't look around, she'll think I didn't hear her and leave me alone. Yes, I'm not above avoiding the problem if I can.

I take a couple quick strides, but Annabel just calls my name again, louder this time, and then she grabs my arm in a surprisingly firm grip. It was wishful thinking anyway. I shrug off her hold and turn around.

"Yes?" I ask, keeping my face bland.

She narrows her eyes at me, probably trying to figure out if I'd been ignoring her on purpose. When I just stare back at her, giving her nothing, she decides not to push it.

"I need you to get stuff together for dinner. And see if you can mend this shirt for me—there's a hole along one side."

She tosses her shirt at me, but I don't even try to catch it. It hits me in the chest and falls to the ground.

"What are you doing?" she snaps, bending down to pick up the shirt. "That was just washed!"

Yeah. By me. That's it. I'm done with all of this. I've been thinking ever since my talk with Gomul, trying to figure out if I really want to do this, how I want to do this, but Annabel just helped me decide.

I'm doing this and I'm going to be direct about it. I look past Annabel to see the other women trying to look like they haven't heard every word so far.

Perfect.

"You know, I think we need to take a group vote on who wants to leave and who wants to stay," I announce, making sure to project my voice.

I look back over at Annabel and meet her eyes head on. It's a brazen move and not at all pre-planned. But I don't know if there is a plan that would avoid conflict.

Annabel is extremely sensitive to any perceived slight to her authority. Though maybe sensitive isn't exactly the right word. Maybe saying she's on a hair trigger would be more accurate.

If we were living in medieval times back on Earth, I don't think it would be much of an exaggeration to say disagreeing with her would have resulted in a swift beheading. Or maybe in being drawn and quartered. For once, I guess we're lucky we aren't on Earth. And that I really don't give a shit at that moment.

I watch in fascination as her face slowly turns beet red, her expression twisting into a tight scowl. She looks like she's going to blow.

Even as I wait for her explosive reaction, the rush of standing up to her is heady. Adrenaline courses through my veins, making me feel truly alive for the first time in too long. I'm so pumped that I don't just leave it at that one comment, like I maybe should. If she's going to be mad anyway, might as well let everything out.

I don't even wait for her response. I decide to keep going.

"You know Annabel, I am so sick of your shit." I hear more than one gasp from the peanut gallery watching. "I'm tired of your pettiness, your lack of ability to listen to anyone else's ideas, and your constant insults. Not only are you grating on the nerves, I don't think you're a good leader. All you're doing is taking the path of least resistance and trying to bully all of us into following along even if it's not the right path." I take a step towards her, using my extra couple inches of height to look down on her as she sputters, so enraged she can't even get a word out. "Well, you know what? I'm done. Completely, permanently done. So. Here's my notice to you —I'm leaving tomorrow." I turn back to all the women watching. "And anyone who wants to come with me is welcome."

There. It's all out there now.

Silence.

I almost expect crickets to start chirping. My stomach starts to tighten with anxiety. I have a moment where I wonder if I'm going to be exiting this place alone. You know, fine. It that's the way it has to be—

"I'm in," cuts in a sure, confident voice. Oh, thank God. It's Fallon. Not much of a surprise, considering that she barely tolerates Annabel at the best of times. She'd been training to serve on the navigation deck of the ship before we crashed, losing her father in the process. Perhaps that contributes to the simmering anger just under the surface, though from what I saw on the ship, he was more of the harsh type.

"Me too." Nora's quiet voice is a bit more surprising. Though if I think about the way Annabel constantly throws insults at her...maybe I shouldn't be so shocked.

"Count me in," Addison adds, standing to join the others. She's more of the brainy, tech-oriented type. She's definitely out of her element here on Tajss. But aren't we all?

"Me as well," Ashlee pipes up, bouncing up with her usual energy. She's a people pleaser who doesn't usually offer much resistance as long as someone else is leading. She has an unflagging positive attitude which is truly impressive considering our circumstances.

"Hope there's room for another," Lanie adds, her tone serious. I nod at her. She's a girly girl and a veterinary expert. She hasn't exactly had a whole lot to study or care for while we've been here, what with all the animals we've encountered so far intent on killing us if they can.

The next one is a real shocker, one that lets me know just how fed up people actually are. Nina takes a deep breath and steps forward.

"I'd like to go as well." I blink at her. Annabel's very own PR consultant? Even she doesn't want to stay anymore?

I stare at the assembled group, all willing to join me in leaving these tunnels and finding out what's out there. I have a team. An actual team! That spark of courage in me grows.

I can do this. *We* can do this.

Annabel finally recovers enough to voice her rage. Yay.

"So all of you are going to run out there to die?" she scoffs. "And you think *she's* going to be able to help you survive?"

"We're all going to help each other survive," I counter.

She shakes her head in disgust.

"I'm leading here," she says fiercely, poking her finger into my chest. I barely resist the urge to slap it away. "And I'm not letting you do this."

"Are we prisoners here then?" Fallon demands, drawing Annabel's attention. "Because that's not what I signed up for."

The others murmur their agreement. She has her there. I

27

can see Annabel mentally back tracking, scrambling for more ways to stop us.

"How are you going to eat?" she demands. "How are you going to find water to drink? How are you going to defend yourself against even one of those monsters out there?"

They are valid points. But not reasons to avoid trying.

"We'll figure it out," I respond.

I don't have to explain myself to her. Those days are over. Her jaw clenches so hard I almost expect to hear her teeth cracking at the pressure.

"Fine. Go." She steps back. "You'll be crawling back here soon enough, begging for my forgiveness," she sneers. "Just remember—if you leave, I might not let you back in."

Does she really think threats are going to stop us at this point?

It's my turn to shake my head in disgust.

"We're heading out first thing tomorrow," I inform her. "Enjoy playing house and leeching from Gomul. You'd be dead without him. It's about time you start respecting that fact instead of treating him like another underling."

By that point, I have no desire to argue with her any further even though she's throwing out more arguments, more insults.

Now that I've made my stand, I have to put my money where my mouth is, which means we need transportation. I really only have one viable option. And after that scene, I'm going to have to make it work.

When the main ship crashed, we were in one of the research pods that were out scouting ahead. We lasted a bit longer than the ship, but eventually we were also forced to lower ourselves into Tajss' atmosphere.

The pod crashed into the sand hard enough that it split in two.

Luckily, the pod also included a land rover I'd designed

and built on the main ship in my earlier engineering days. And wonder of all wonders, it survived the landing mostly intact. After we crashed and managed to fix it, we were able to use it to travel.

Unfortunately, not before the lizard-like beasts that attacked us when we crashed managed to kill a good amount of our group, increasing the casualty count. The men who had survived the impact were all killed when they tried to fight off those animals.

Giant lizards with humping mounds across their back and skin lined with sharp spikes weren't anything we were prepared for, especially not after the shock of the crash. And those things were vicious in their attack.

If Gomul hadn't come out of hiding to help us, we would've all died right then. There's no question. We all owe our lives to him.

I feel a pang in my heart. I'm going to miss Gomul. But it's well past time to move on. I know there must be more of our people out there.

And I honestly don't know how much longer we're going to survive down here underground anyway. All of us are pale, weak, the climate here not one conducive to human health. I don't want to waste away down here. And I can't sit here biting my tongue forever, submitting to the rule of a clear narcissist for the rest of my days on this hunk of rock.

Yeah. It's time to go.

I reach the rover without a problem, where it's parked near the entrance to the tunnels. It needs repairs before we can take it out, so I get to work fixing, checking under the hood, and also checking the wiring underneath along with the actual body of the thing.

While I'm halfway under the vehicle, muttering to myself as I patch up holes torn into the undercarriage, I hear footsteps approach.

"Are we leaving in the morning?" I hear Fallon ask.

"Yes," I respond after a pause. How odd that I'm actually in charge. "I should have this thing ready to go by then. Tell the others to be ready."

"Got it."

I hear the murmur of her voice and others as the footsteps move away again.

All right then. I have the night to make all the fixes I need to. Time to get moving. As with all repairs, it takes me longer than I expected. A bunch of bruises, a cut finger, and a sleepless night later, I finally have it ready to go.

I probably have a couple of hours left for resting before we head out. I should sleep. But before I do that, I need to pay Gomul a visit. I can't leave without seeing him one more time.

He's awake. He doesn't look all that surprised to see me when I arrive in his tunnel.

"I heard you're leaving," he says, watching me.

"What you said...it struck a chord in me," I explain.

It's as simple and complex as that.

He smiles at me.

"I am glad," he says simply. "Though I am sad to see you leave, I think it is the right thing for you to do."

I feel something else ease inside me. Even that little snippet of support makes me feel better about my decision.

"I am glad you came to see me, so I do not have to find you. I have drawn a rough map for you that will take you near food plants," he explains, picking up a rolled-up piece of hide nearby. After unrolling it, he points out what all the symbols mean. "You cannot fell any of the beasts here, so you will have to rely on the growing food. I have also marked water sources you can use on your journey." He looks up at me. "I know with these resources, you will be successful in your endeavor."

"Thank you, Gomul," I murmur, shaking my head, completely overwhelmed at the show of support and the help. The map will be more than helpful out there in the harsh desert—it could even save our lives.

He inclines his head.

"I have also packed some food for you and your group," he adds, gesturing to the laden bags to the side that I hadn't paid much attention to.

"Gomul! That's your food!" I exclaim, shaking my head. "We've already taken enough—"

"Nonsense," he interrupts. "I have enough. And you will need the resources." His eyes are kind as he leans towards me. "You are a leader now. You must think of those in your care as well." He looks over at the food. "You will need to ration it carefully. If you do, you should be able to survive on that alone for perhaps three weeks."

I nod, considering his words before I refuse again. He's right. I have a group to take care of now. I cannot deny the help.

"Thank you," I murmur again, humbled. "You don't know how much this means to me."

"You will need to be firm," he warns. "They are your wards first now—friends second."

He has to repeat that last sentence for me, explain it until I understand he means those in my charge. I've learned his language pretty well, but there are still words I don't know. Once I understand the sentiment, the thought is sobering. He's right. I'm going to have to shift mental gears to lead.

I sit with Gomul a little longer as I contemplate that. I don't know when I will see him again, after all. This time is precious. When I finally leave to take a nap, I give him a tight hug, one he returns gingerly.

"Safe journey," he murmurs.

I nod, blinking back tears. And resolve to visit him again,

if at all possible. The nap I manage to take recharges me enough to continue forward when combined with the nerves and adrenaline that are also riding me.

When I'm up off the pallet again, I load up the rover with the food Gomul was nice enough to provide and tuck the map securely in the driver's side.

Then I give the rover one more go-over, not wanting to find out I missed something after we're already out of here.

When I get under the thing, I'm glad I did. There's a problem with the wiring that I hadn't noticed the night bef—

I take a closer look. My lips tighten as anger surges through me. Someone deliberately opened the protective casing for some of the electrical wiring and cut the wires on the surface. It's a hatchet job.

I take a deep breath to calm myself.

I don't need three guesses to have a pretty good idea who it was. Is this really what it's come to? Is she this power hungry, this petty that she would sabotage our only vehicle just to keep us here? I shake my head as I get to work repairing the wires. We were lucky, in a way. Annabel doesn't know anything about tech or engineering or she could have done something that would have taken a lot longer to fix. Or something that would have been irreparable under these conditions. As it is, this is really just an inconvenience.

It takes me about forty minutes to undo the damage and close the protective casing back up. By the time I'm done and sliding out from under the vehicle again, my group is arranged around the rover.

Along with a bunch of the others, Annabel in the lead.

"Is it ready to go?" Addison asks, glancing at the rover with a critical eye.

I nod, wiping my hands as I look at Annabel.

"Sure is," I say, my tone sardonic as I raise a brow at her.

Her jaw clenches.

"If you leave, don't come back," she snarls.

With that parting shot, she spins around and shoves her way through the crowd to stalk away.

Those staying look at each other uneasily. Good luck to them. I can only hope Annabel will calm down and realize she's hurting the people she should be taking care of. And that she might lose more of them if she doesn't change something.

"Come on," I say quietly. "Let's head out."

Everyone moves forward to store their bags in the back, and then we climb in.

The rover starts at the first touch and I maneuver it out. We've been mostly underground for some time now in those tunnels. In fact, it's been...

It's been years.

The realization is like a kick to the stomach. We should have left the tunnels ages ago. I should've seen that we needed to leave well before this. I shouldn't have needed Gomul's kick in the pants.

I shake my head at myself. It doesn't matter. We're leaving now. There's no point in looking to the past.

I hear hisses from inside the rover as we come out into the full, burning light of the two suns. I drive slowly, narrowing my eyes as I try to adjust to the light after the dimness of the tunnels.

"Man, that's ridiculously bright," Lanie comments. "I feel like a mole rat finally leaving its hole."

Mutters of agreement follow that statement. She isn't far off from the truth. We've been down there, out of the sunlight, for way too long.

Without a specific destination in mind, I pull out the map. Might as well follow the planned route Gomul formed for us.

"Here goes nothing," I say under my breath.

I drive forward. And keep driving. We only stop to go to

33

the bathroom and eat. There isn't somewhere we have to be at a certain time, but the more ground we cover the better if we're trying to explore and see what's out here.

The day passes with wave after wave of the red sandy dunes this planet is covered in. The suns never cease their glaring shine and it feels like any direction we go in looks basically the same. Boredom settles in quite quickly, prompting a couple of the girls to ask if they can snack on the food we have.

"Can we have a little more of the dried meat?" Ashlee asks.

Nora voices her agreement.

With Gomul's voice still clear in my mind, I refuse.

"We have to be really careful with our supplies," I explain. "If we don't overindulge, they should last us a few weeks."

"I thought Gomul told you where we could find food?" Nina asks.

"He did," I confirm. "But we don't know what we're going to find when we get to those places. I don't know how long it's been since he's actually visited them all."

Or what danger could be lurking there when we arrive, though I don't mention that last worry. They finally subside, realizing I'm not going to give in here. Though they bring up the issue again. Multiple times. I know none of us are really full, but we've had enough food to last us, considering we're not walking but simply driving. Some of them want more just for comfort, so I hold strong. I need to make sure we have enough food to last us. That's my priority.

As more time passes, we alternate drivers so we can keep moving even during the night. Seeing the predators we already have, staying still for a prolonged period of time doesn't seem like a great idea.

So that's how we continue for the next couple of days. We haven't found anything interesting by that point, but I'm glad that at the very least, we're out of those tunnels and in the open. I feel like I can finally breathe again. But the smooth sailing doesn't last for long.

"We have company," Fallon calls out urgently from the back on our third day out.

I glance in the rear-view mirror and at the screen that shows the camera view behind us. I frown.

"I don't see..."

There's a flicker of movement over one of the distant dunes.

"It looks like the same things that attacked us before," Lanie chimes in, her tone tight. "Maybe three of them?"

Shit. That is not good.

"Let's see how much juice we can get out of this thing," I mutter, pushing down on the accelerator.

The rover lurches forward. I push hard, as fast as I can safely drive. When we stop, it's only to take care of our needs. Then it's back in the rover to eat as we speed away again.

"They're gaining," Lanie informs me. "At least, one is. That's the only one I can still see."

When I look back this time, I see the thing crest the dune right behind the one we just traversed. That same giant lizard-like thing, with thick skin and a humped back, deadly spikes growing out of it at various spots. Its teeth are razor sharp. I know that from the attack when we first landed. The men hadn't stood a chance against them.

I take a deep breath. That isn't going to be us. I refuse to let it be.

But Lanie's right. It's going to be upon us soon. We have to change strategies here. I stare at it, judging its size. If I wait for it to catch up to us, it could do a lot of damage to the rover. Without the rover, we're easy prey out here. I glance around, not seeing any convenient cover anywhere nearby. Just like I haven't for the last hundred miles.

We have only one option here really. I slow the car down.

"What are you doing?" Fallon asks sharply. "We need to get farther away, not closer."

"We're not going to be able to outrun it," I explain, pointing out the obvious. "We have to try something else."

"So we're just going to let it catch us?" Addison asks, her voice rising with fear. "And what? Tell it to stop?"

"No," I say calmly, jamming the gear into reverse. "We're going to take it out before it can take us out."

"Oh my God," Nora mutters.

"It's a good a plan as any," Fallon muses.

"Glad you approve." I look back at everyone. "Brace yourselves, guys."

Everyone grabs hold of what they can, their seat belts already fastened.

"Ready?"

The nods I receive are varied, none of them completely sure. Good enough.

I look back. The thing is just at the top of the dune directly behind us. I stopped the rover at the top of the one we're on. Perfect.

I take a deep breath.

And gun it.

We shoot backwards, a couple of the others let out screams. The acceleration is amplified by the downhill path we're taking. We're going fast. Really fast.

"Come on," I mutter as I see the thing still moving towards us.

We need to hit it with a high enough speed that we kill it. And I'm only going to have one chance at this. If I don't get it the first time, I won't have the chance to set up a second shot as good as this one.

The thing starts to move to the side as we near, but it isn't quite fast enough.

We're braced for it, but the impact is still jarring.

More shrieks come from the back as we fall into a spin, metal squealing and sand flying as the world rotates around us. I'm holding on so tightly I can't feel my hands. We finally come to a stop some yards away.

Am I still in one piece?

I swallow, slowly prying my fingers off the bar on the door. I feel like my heart might have stopped for a second there. I clear my throat.

"Is...is everyone all right?" I ask, my voice hoarse. Had I been screaming too?

"Yeah."

"Uh huh."

"I think so?"

Everyone confirms they are indeed alive and in one piece.

"What about the guster?" I ask next, trying to orient myself.

Spinning a few times at high speed is...disorienting.

"Can't see it," Fallon mutters.

The others confirm.

"All right."

The best thing to do is drive over there and check. I try to turn the rover on. I try again.

"Is something wrong?" Addison asks.

I sigh, leaning my head on the steering wheel.

"I think the speed we needed blew a fuse."

I hit my head against the wheel. This is not what we need. But I can't just sit and wallow.

First order of business—check on the guster.

"I'll be right back."

"Wait—"

"Where are you going?"

I step out of the car and shield my eyes to look over the sand. The path the car took is clear—the tires leaving a circular track pattern. Well, several circles. I don't hear anything. I take a deep breath and let it out. Here goes nothing. I feel like that's fast becoming my motto.

I trudge across the dune, following the tracks. The sooner we know, the better. If it's about to attack us, I'll be gone first. Not great. But at least they'll have some warning.

I hear another door open behind me.

"Stay inside while I check," I call back. No use in all of us taking this risk.

Edging to the left, I stop abruptly. The thing is in view now, and it isn't moving. Upon closer examination, it looks like I was successful in bashing its head right in. It's leaking...

I swallow the bile that wants to come up.

I turn back to the car but stop when I see the others already walking towards me.

"I told you to wait in the car," I point out.

"We couldn't leave you to fend for yourself," Fallon points out.

"And I could probably tell better if it's actually dead..." Lanie trails off as she catches sight of the body. "Yep. That's dead all right."

I snort.

"Very helpful." I shake my head. "Okay, we shouldn't let all this meat go to waste. We need to break it down and store it for later. While you take care of that, I'm going to go check on the rover, see if I can fix it."

"Aye aye, Captain," Fallon says cheekily, throwing me a salute.

"I'll come with you," Addison pipes up. "In case you need another opinion."

I nod. Any help would be appreciated, and Addison knows her away around tech, if not this rover in particular. Some basics could overlap.

Leaving the rest to start in on the guster, we head back to

the rover. The actual body of the vehicle is only slightly dented from the impact, and I used the back deliberately to protect the engine.

I'm pretty sure it was the speed we used that killed it. Wow. We killed a guster on our own. And now we have meat too. If the rover was still working, I would have called this whole thing a definite win.

After sinking down to the hot sand, I ignore the heat and shimmy underneath the vehicle. I open the protective casing and carefully check everything. It isn't a fuse. It's likely another component, a vital one. I'll have to check under the hood to make sure, but it can only be a couple things. Shimmying out, I walk to the front to open the hood.

It doesn't take long to find the problem. I touch the singed area. I'm going to have to weld it to fix it. How, I don't know quite yet.

"Want to give me a second opinion, Addison?" I ask quietly.

She shakes her head.

"Welding," she confirms.

I sigh.

"Yeah."

Well, we've diagnosed the problem. I just don't know how to work around this. We have to figure it out. We can't just stay here immobile. We're like sitting ducks.

"Kate! Kate!"

I almost hit my head on the hood as I hear the others shouting my name. Cursing, I close the hood just in time for Ashlee to run over.

"What? What is it?"

She tries to catch her breath as she points ahead.

"There. There's another Zmaj heading this way," she gasps.

What? A Zmaj? My heart beat picks up again as I follow her finger. Maybe she's wrong...

I squint into the distance. I feel my back tighten.

There. Wings, tail... She's right.

"What do we do?" she asks anxiously.

I shake my head. I have no idea what to expect. Gomul was amazing and continues to be great. But he also warned us, said we were fortunate we didn't run into some others. He never gave specifics on who to avoid and this is the first time I really regret that.

"Come on," I urge Addison and Ashlee. "Let's join the rest."

I'll feel safer with all of us together, though I don't know if that's actually true. None of us can fight someone like Gomul and win.

We make it to the rest of our group just as the new Zmaj lands, traveling much faster than we can. He's built for this crazy planet.

When he lands, I have to tilt my head back to meet his eyes. He's tall. Maybe even taller than Gomul. Definitely younger. With broad shoulders and a muscular build, he's even more imposing. And eye-catching. His scales are an almost peacock blue-green, glowing brightly in the sunlight. And the bright blue green eyes set in his handsome face match.

My eyes lock on his as I force myself to walk towards him. He's...entrancing. I feel that undeniable sizzle of chemistry, my skin a little too tight, a little too sensitive. But that doesn't matter.

I will myself past the obvious fact that I'm attracted to this large, bipedal dragon. But I can't push past something even more odd. I feel like...

Like I can trust him. How absolutely ridiculous is that? Almost as ridiculous as being attracted to a dragon.

He watches intently as I stop a few feet away and then introduces himself.

"I am Errol."

Errol.

"Pleasure to make your acquaintance, Errol," I return, tasting the name. "I'm Kate."

It isn't nearly as exotic and pretty. How appropriate.

4

ERROL

*T*his encounter is one I never could have predicted. What if I hadn't volunteered to deliver the order to the city? I might never have encountered the most beautiful female I have ever laid my eyes upon.

I know I am staring, but I cannot look away. Her hair is a red brighter than the sands of the desert, and her skin is so pale it is almost translucent. Her delicate, pretty face is dominated by large gray eyes and a soft pink mouth. This close, I can see a shift of iridescence in those eyes, drawing me in even further.

Her gaze is direct and clear, and I suddenly feel as though she can see right into me. I wonder if she can feel how that gaze sends my heartbeat racing. It's not only because she is beautiful, which she is. It's also because of the presence she has due to her personality, which she doesn't try to hide, as some females do. The fact that she is the group's leader is obvious. Of course, anyone could tell when she stepped forward to greet me, but it's also there in her demeanor. Strong, confident. Ready to defend her small group of females from me if necessary.

I need to show that I am no threat. Forcing myself to look away from Kate, I survey her group. They all vary in their coloring and heights, but they are all thin and washed out. Pale. I glance at Kate. She is too, though I did not realize that in the beginning, so taken was I with her beauty.

I frown, looking behind them at their vehicle. It is not Zmaj technology. And it is parked at a slant on a hill, which is not a safe place to park on the unstable sands of Tajss. Something must be wrong with it.

"Can I be of assistance?" I inquire, looking back at Kate after my quick survey.

She sighs, glancing back to the vehicle as well.

"Do you have electricity I can use to weld together the parts that are fried?" she asks.

"Fried?" I ask. I believe I know what she means. Her language skills are quite good though the phrasing is somewhat off. She has obviously had contact with other Zmaj. "How did that happen?"

"We had to kill a guster," she explains.

I raise my brows at that.

"A guster?" I repeat.

She nods, gesturing to the side.

"We've managed to break it down for meat..."

I walk over and see a dead guster, already stripped for meat as she stated. I nod, impressed.

"That is a good reason to accidentally break your vehicle," I agree, shaking my head. Kate is only more intriguing the longer I speak to her. "As for the welding, we have technology in the city that may be useful."

She quirks a brow, a wash of surprise spreading across her face. Does she not know of the city? How have they survived this long here? Even if I don't take into account that she can speak the Zmaj language, they can't have survived on their own since the crash. Tajss is a harsh place. Especially for humans. Humans who are clearly weakened like these females are. They are easy prey.

"A city..." she mutters.

Turning to the females watching, hovering nearby at the ready, she calms them with a gentle but firm voice.

"It's okay. I think he can help us—he's mentioned a city."

The others exclaim, glancing at each other. She speaks to them in the now-familiar human tongue. I wonder if she realizes I can understand her. As she speaks to her group, I see them calming, the respect and trust they have for Kate clear. It shows in their eyes, in their body language. Kate is a natural leader, her own centered energy giving them an anchor with which to stabilize their own emotions. They do not fear her. That much is also clear. They simply trust her to lead, trust she will do what is best. A true sign of an admirable leader.

But where did she come from?

When she turns back to me, I ask her how many of them survived. I can see her guard rising at the question.

"We were in a research pod...a small ship," she explains when I cock my head. "But after the main ship crashed, we couldn't stay up for long. I'm certain there are at least two other pods that couldn't have survived outside of the ship for more than a short time period before their fuel ran out. So they must have crashed too."

Interesting. She does not seem to be aware of any survivors other than those of her own pod. And I am aware that she does not actually mention how many of them survived.

"I know of your ship. In fact, there are many from it who have come to live in the city."

Her face brightens as the females behind her cry out in excitement, having crept closer to hear us more clearly. She looks back at them, sharing their joy at the news.

"That's wonderful," she says, turning back to me with a smile that warms me inside. I like that I was able to put it there. "We thought maybe..."

She shakes her head, clearly overwhelmed at the news.

"I can lead you there if you like," I offer gently, wanting to take her in my arms, offer her comfort.

But that is too forward. She does not know me. Not yet. I take a deep breath, turning my head, ostensibly to study the non-functional vehicle, but really just to look away from her. From Kate. From her luminous skin and her bright hair, that confidence in her gaze—I bite back a growl of arousal. I cannot show it. It will only scare her away, and that I do not want. Taking a deep breath, I attempt to behave as my normal self.

"We'd like that very much," Kate agrees.

I glance back at her, my eyes meeting her grateful gray ones. I nod, looking away again. My eyes focus on the large vehicle this time—the rover, that was what she called it. My inner craftsman rises to the fore as I walk over to it.

Kate walks alongside me.

"The hood is over here," she explains, moving over and gesturing at it. "Here..." She helps me lift the flat metal portion covering the engine and then starts to point out the seared, blacked section. "I need to weld here and here to get it working again. I just need the tools."

She wants me to know she is self-sufficient for the most part, that she knows how to fix the vehicle, but is simply lacking the resources. I admire her for that. Many of the human females I have met are resourceful, eager to learn, and strong enough to maintain their sanity under the conditions they have found themselves in. I respect all of them for good reason. But this is different. I am intrigued in a different way, on a different level.

"I believe we will find the tools you need in the city."

"That would be great." She meets my eyes for a moment, something flickering in their depths. But she does not stay so close for long. "I should get the others ready."

As she pulls back and starts tossing out orders to the others to prepare for the journey ahead, I know this feeling spells something far deeper than simple attraction. Something I am compelled to pursue.

I move back from the vehicle as the humans set to packing the essentials they have stored inside. Kate stands back to direct. I come to stand beside her, leaving a comfortable distance so she does not feel crowded.

"Where are you traveling from?" I ask, attempting to engage her in more conversation, learn more about their time on Tajss.

Her eyes flick over to me.

"From that direction," she says, vaguely pointing. "We've been staying underground, in tunnels we found after we crashed."

This is the first I have heard of any humans in tunnels. I nod thoughtfully. "It is fortunate you were able to find shelter before the creatures of Tajss found you," I say.

"I..." She frowns, but then nods. "Yes. It is."

"Is this how you find food to eat?" I ask, gesturing to where the guster lies. "You hit it with your vehicle?"

Another flicker of expression, there and gone. She shrugs. "There are also herbs and other things in and around the tunnels. We managed." She walks away, clearly wanting to end the conversation.

I frown at her back. There is no doubt there is something she is not mentioning. Perhaps...someone? Or perhaps multiple someones. But I do not begrudge her that. I understand wanting to protect the people she cares about from a stranger.

I look forward to gaining her trust, to having her confide

in me. For the first time in a long time, I feel a spark of life reignite in my heart. A surge of excitement. Something to look forward to each day beyond the simple joy of craftsmanship I bring to the Tribe.

This is more personal. This is a deeper hope. And I welcome it.

5

KATE

"Don't take anything that isn't essential," I warn. "Walking out here in the desert is no joke even without a pack. And if all goes well, we'll come back to get the rover in any case."

I plan to anyway. That rover is like my baby. I built it from the ground up on the generational ship and I'm proud of it. The workmanship speaks for itself. Even after the crash, the intentionally low-tech design has held up. The fuel converter uses solar receivers and trash to power the vehicle and the heavy-duty materials used to make it are tough enough to, say, kill a guster and survive. Mostly. It really is the best option for the hard terrain here on Tajss. A happy accident. We could use more of those.

I quickly help divide up the food and water we can carry.

"Ready?" I ask, after I see everyone has rolled up their belongings.

I get nods all around. All right, good to go.

I look over at Errol. It's difficult to not stare at him the whole time, honestly, but I manage not to embarrass myself. At least, not yet.

"We're good to go," I tell him, adjusting my own pack.

He nods. "This way."

Errol is obviously built for this place, his wings giving him some lift, so he doesn't sink into the sand. We're not nearly as graceful as we trudge along behind him, but we manage. At least we make forward progress, but I do immediately miss the rover. I want to sigh from the bottom of my lungs, but I'm learning to control stuff like that because my emotions affect the other women. In my head, I curse the guster for wrecking my rover. Then again, if we hadn't used the rover on the guster, we might not even be alive to complain about this trek now. And I wouldn't have met Errol.

He slows, walking along beside me for a bit, but then he moves ahead again.

"I will scout ahead to look for any possible trouble," he says and gives me a smile that makes my heart speed up.

The scouting will be much appreciated by our whole group. I feel a lot safer with someone who knows Tajss with us.

So that's how we travel. He mostly stays in the lead, getting a good look at the area ahead of us. Occasionally, I catch up with him. Even more rarely, I actually pass him by, enjoying the surprise on his face when I do. I'm competitive by nature though, and the playful competition helps keep me motivated under the searing sun. But I still maintain my distance from him for the most part. I'm still not sure about him—the vague gut feeling that tells me I can trust him isn't enough to throw all caution to the wind. Especially when I'm not just responsible for myself.

I glance back at the group from time to time, to make sure everyone is accounted for. We're all exhausted pretty early on. The heat, the sun, the sinking sand—it's a lot. And we didn't start our journey in what I'd call top physical condition. I didn't realize exactly how weak we'd all gotten until this moment. Though it isn't surprising that we haven't exactly been thriving on this inhospitable alien planet. We're lucky we're even alive at all. We keep walking at that relatively slow pace until night starts to fall.

"We will break for food and rest here," Errol says, slowing to walk beside me. He points at a hollowed-out ridge that offers some protection.

I nod. Sounds like a good plan. And I'm definitely ready to sit. I pass the information down to the rest of the group, and we all head over to the space Errol pointed out. I groan along with the others as we set down our belongings and sit down. My legs and back are aching with the unaccustomed exercise.

"You should have some water," Errol murmurs, lowering himself down to sit next to me. "Food will also help. Your people are not adapted to the desert."

I chuckle at that understatement.

"Yes," I agree, taking his advice and having a sip of water. "This is not our natural...place."

I don't know how to say environment, but Errol seems to catch the drift of what I'm trying to say.

"It is a hard place, Tajss," he agrees. He looks out over the expanse of desert. "But it is home."

I nod, pulling out my portion of the rations without a verbal response. I don't really want to fall into a conversation with him. In fact, I've been trying my best to avoid it this whole time. This draw I feel for him, this desire to trust him... It leaves me off-kilter. Better to keep him at a bit of a distance until I get a handle on it.

Luckily, he seems to sense my desire for distance just fine. Even better, he doesn't push it, simply settling down to eat next to me in companionable silence. How refreshing. I appreciate his respect for my wishes, for my boundaries. Not everyone is so accommodating.

Forcing myself to look away, I focus on my water and food. I am pretty damned ravenous, so it actually isn't as difficult as it might have been. I probably don't look all that attractive while I scarf down the food and guzzle my water, but there you go. The fact that I even consider how I look at that moment is a glaring indicator that I want Errol to like how I look. I shake my head at myself. That's a little embarrassing. Especially when I know I look a mess from the day of traveling on foot.

When I'm done downing the food so inelegantly, I regret it for a different reason. Now I have no excuse not to talk. The silence turns a little odd as we sit there. Great.

"So...uh...do you live in the city?" I ask.

Errol shakes his head, also having finished eating. Though he was a lot more polite about it than I was.

"No, I live with my Tribe, though we are allies. In fact, I was just traveling back home from the city when I encountered your group."

"Oh." I consider that. "I'm sorry for messing up your plans." He frowns at me. "Uh...interrupting...your plans?" I try.

My grasp on the language is a lot better than it used to be, but we only really had Gomul to talk to.

"Ah." His face clears. "It is really no trouble—"

A feminine scream rips through the night air, shrill and frightened.

Errol and I both jump up.

"Ashlee went to use the bathroom," Lanie says urgently, her eyes wide.

"Which way?" I demand.

She points a shaky finger.

Errol takes off instantly, going much faster than I can. I

scramble after him, my heart beating fast. I've seen some of the creatures here. What if we don't get there quickly enough?

Errol flares his wings and leaps over the dune at the top of the ridge, his powerful body making it look easy. I shove myself over much more slowly, probably looking like an idiot, but I'm more concerned with speed than how I look.

Especially when Ashlee screams again.

When I get to the top and have my first look at the situation, my heart freezes in my chest. Ashlee is running towards us, and the thing behind her is gaining. What the hell is that?!

It's massive and vaguely gorilla-like in appearance, with bulging arms and huge fists that it uses to help propel itself forward. Thick fur flies back as it runs forward, the long strands covering its shoulders and the top half of its arms. I can't be sure in the dimmer light, but the bare skin of its forearms looks blue. Can that be right?

Its dark eyes are focused on Ashlee, and even bent over like it is, it's about as tall as she is. It's clearly much stronger than any of us. It's also clear just how lucky we are that Errol is here right now.

He jumps from the top of the dune, brandishing his lochaber, the same kind of long-handled, bladed weapon Gomul uses. His wings flare out, his tail whipping behind him as he swings the blade to the side, soaring directly over Ashlee. With a smooth, hard rotation, he slashes at the thing's face with the blade. The beast stumbles back, shrieking and covering its face.

Errol is magnificent. He takes control of the situation. His movements are smooth, almost cat-like in their speed and decisiveness. He strikes at the thing again, avoiding a swing of those powerful fists, cutting another slash into the creature's muscled chest. He strikes boldly, with precision and force that I can tell surprise the beast. It was expecting to take only Ashlee. Easy prey.

Ashlee reaches me then, her breathing harsh. I grab her, trying to calm her as she also turns to watch.

Errol is mesmerizing as he dodges and weaves around the creature, deliberately keeping its attention away from us. He reminds me of the old nineteen-eighties sword and sorcery heroes. Wings and muscles rippling, eyes filled with a determined, fierce fury that would strike fear in anything sentient. Anything sentient that had an ounce of intelligence that is.

However, the beast he's fighting is literally foaming at the mouth, something I didn't realize earlier. It looks like it's out of control, not thinking completely clearly. Otherwise, it would have retreated already, clearly outclassed by Errol. But that doesn't mean it isn't dangerous.

As Errol extends his arm, spinning his lochaber back around, the creature manages to slash at his arm with its claws right before the blade slices halfway through its thick neck.

I cry out in dismay, taking a step towards the fight, though I don't know what I think I can do to help. It moved more quickly than a thing of that girth looked like it could. But that last blow Errol deals is the fatal one. The creature continues moving forward, but it is already dead on its feet. Errol shifts to the side and it falls forward to the ground, its large body sprawling over the sand, dark blood soaking in a growing pool around the neck wound.

"Wow."

I glance over at the word. The rest of our group is arranged along the crest of the dune around us, all staring at the dead animal. I don't even know when they arrived, I was so focused on the action.

Errol rises from his crouch, stepping away from the

thing, his chest rising and falling quickly with harsh breaths. He looks up at us. I almost take a step back.

"I believe we should move on to the closest water source," he says, his voice harsh, his eyes still holding the intensity of the fight. "Majmun are pack animals. I do not know why this one is alone in the desert, away from the trees they usually dwell in. Perhaps it is simply crazed. Perhaps it is simply like the other animals that were recently disturbed by the meteorite showers. But I do not want to run into the rest of his pack if it is nearby."

I nod immediately. Sound logic. I turn to the group.

"Pack up. Let's get the hell out of here."

No one argues with that. We hustle hard and we're packed up and ready to go within five minutes.

Errol leads us again, directly to a small oasis about a half hour away. At least the suns are close to setting now, so the journey doesn't feel as difficult. Probably the shock of adrenaline we just had also helps.

"Oh, thank God. Water."

"Man, I could really use a bath."

"Yeah, you really could."

"Shut up!"

I smile at the teasing back and forth as spirits lift again.

The sight of water is really welcome after the day we've had. It occurs to me that I have never seen a natural body of water in my entire life. The spring, sparkling with the last of the sunset light, and the trees, whose leaves flutter in a light breeze, are the most beautiful things I've seen in years. I feel tears gather in my eyes. The other women are standing nearby. Are they feeling the same?

Errol does a quick scout of the spring and the trees around it before giving us the go ahead, his eyes sharp and watchful. He's been on guard this whole time, but the encounter with the creature has him appearing even sharper.

Just like the rest of us. Nothing like an attack to keep you on your toes.

The other girls rush forward, stripping down to their underwear and jumping into the water with cries of delight. I turn to Errol, who's eyes are constantly scanning around us, looking for threats.

"Come on, Errol," I murmur, taking his hand in mine. He starts at the touch, his eyes shifting to me. "Let's get you cleaned up too. That thing got you good."

"Majmun," he says, allowing me to guide him to the water.

"Maj-moon?" I repeat, turning his arm to get a better look at the gouges. They're bleeding. At the very least they need to be cleaned.

"Yes. Majmun," he says, watching as I rip off the bottom of my shirt. "What are you doing?"

"Taking care of your wound," I explain, crouching down to dip my shirt in the water. It's already cooling a bit with the suns setting.

When I rise back up, he stays still, watching as I carefully clean his arm. I know it must hurt, but he doesn't move, his eyes focused unflinchingly on my face. Like he might let me do anything to him. The thought sends a thrill through me that I quickly suppress.

I look away to wring out the shirt, but then meet his eyes again. His gaze is...electrifying. I swallow as I smooth the cloth over his skin. It's like the fight tore away a piece of that civilized exterior. Leaving someone more...naked. More primal.

My heartbeat increases for a different reason now. Whatever this is, between us? It's not something I can ignore. Not something I can deny. Do I even want to try?

6

ERROL

"WHAT is that gleam over there?" Kate asks, wiping the sweat from her eyes.

"Our destination," I smile, giving her a hand as she climbs the last few steps to crest of the dune.

A softly muttered "Oh," is her only response.

Traveling on, my wards are mostly silent, focusing on putting one foot in front of the other. Their bodies do not travel well at all and the closer we get to the City the more the land becomes rolling dunes of loose sand. Every step they take they sink in, sometimes half way to their knees. Their lack of wings and tail leave them unable to move quickly.

It takes most of the day before we're climbing to the top of the final dune. Kate stops beside me, clearly shocked. I can understand why. From what I have gleaned, they have only seen the desert and the tunnels they took shelter in after they crash-landed. The city is a sight to behold for anyone, even for me. It's a testament to Zmaj technology, to the heights we reached at our peak, before the Devastation and the downfall of our society.

The shimmering dome that covers the entirety of it reflects the suns brilliantly. Inside the dome are the towering buildings that were once known as Drakonov. One of the larger cities on Tajss and one of the only ones, as far as I know, that survived the Devastation.

The females gasp, oohing and ahhing. Kate shivers, turning towards me, moisture glinting in her eyes.

"It's beautiful," she says, her voice barely above a whisper and my heart leaps in my chest.

I don't have words to respond. Her emotions are so strong they brush against me like the soft touch of the wind. Swallowing hard I nod and then help her as we start down the last dune to the dome.

I get us through the dome that protects the city and its inhabitants and then guide my wards through to Rosalind. She is the undisputed leader here and her office is where our first stop needs to be. As we walk, the females look around with wide eyes, talking to each other in low voices. We don't encounter many people as we walk through, though we do get some curious glances from those who see us. Nobody stops us, however.

Luckily, Rosalind is in her office when we arrive, and I do not have to force the group to walk the entire city. They are clearly exhausted. Rosalind's assistant gives our group one look and immediately rushes to inform her of our presence.

"So Rosalind is in charge of the entire city?" Kate asks in a hushed voice.

"Yes. She has shown herself to be a strong and logical leader."

Kate makes a thoughtful sound. "That does sound like Rosalind."

I hear the murmur of conversation beyond the door and then it bursts open to reveal the leader herself. She's a beautiful woman with long dark hair, usually calm and measured in her demeanor. But I see a different Rosalind today. Surprise and joy suffuse her face as she sees Kate and the others.

"Kate!" she cries out, rushing forward.

Kate laughs, meeting her halfway, embracing Rosalind with just as much enthusiasm.

I blink.

It seems there will be no need to persuade Rosalind to give aid to Kate and her group.

Rosalind draws back from the hug, looking behind Kate at the others. The fierce and controlled woman slowly starts to return.

"How many survived from your pod?" she asks, frowning. Ah—it is clear she would have expected more than this small group. Perhaps I will also hear more answers now that Rosalind is the one asking.

"We survived the initial crash landing," Kate says, the happiness and excitement slowly leaving her expression and tone. "But then we were attacked by guster. None of the men survived that. Those that didn't die in the initial attack succumbed to their wounds within weeks without proper medical care available."

The normally stoic leader appears stricken at the news.

"None of them?" she whispers. "Karim, Mateo, Ji-hoon...?"

Kate shakes her head, her eyes sad.

"No. I'm sorry. I know you were close," she murmurs.

Rosalind nods, her face pale. I feel my own heart ache in sympathy. I know there is a difference between knowing intellectually that someone is most likely gone and having it confirmed. She is silent for a few moments, processing the news. But she is strong, collecting herself and refocusing on the matter at hand. I would expect no less given my experience with Rosalind so far.

"How did you manage to sustain yourselves?" she asks, meeting all their eyes. "Up until this very moment, I thought the pods had returned to the docking bay and went down with the ship..."

"It was difficult," Kate says carefully, suddenly a bit more closed off. "We found shelter in some underground tunnels where we were mostly protected. Annabel and the others stayed behind there. They didn't think it was safe to venture out." She smiles wryly. "They weren't wrong about the danger."

So there are others, but she is still avoiding something. That is not the entirety of their experience here. Rosalind frowns slightly. I think she senses Kate is withholding something from her. But Kate's expression remains only attentive in the face of the scrutiny, not giving anything away. I am more certain Kate is hiding something than Rosalind seems to be, sensing it more keenly than she does, for some reason. I feel more in tune with Kate than I should after so short an acquaintance, but that does not change the fact that the connection is there.

In any case, Kate has not been in the city long enough to start confessing all her secrets regarding how she and the other females survived. Perhaps she will once she feels more comfortable here, once she concludes it is safe. I can see that Rosalind is about to ask more questions. And Kate does as well.

"Is there any lodging available for us here?" she asks, diverting the other woman's attention and forestalling the line of questioning before it can continue.

Rosalind's face clears.

"Of course. And we have food for you as well." She casts a measuring eye over the thin, pale group. "It looks like you could use both the food and the rest."

"I'm not going to disagree with you on that," Kate agrees, the rest of the group nodding tiredly.

"I can show them to one of the common areas," I volunteer. "And arrange their rooms." I will take any reasonable excuse I can to be close to Kate.

"That would be appreciated. Thank you, Errol." She turns back to Kate. "We'll speak more once you have had a chance to rest and eat."

Kate smiles back and nods, stepping away.

"Sounds good."

That obligation fulfilled, I lead them out of the office and to the center of the city, directly to one of the smaller common areas. There is always food available there, though it isn't a usual meal time now. I manage to gather enough up for everyone.

"Thanks, Errol," Fallon says gratefully, making up her plate.

"Second that. I'm so glad to be eating inside. And not in a tunnel at that," Addison adds.

The others add in their agreement.

"You are welcome," I return with a smile, settling in next to Kate.

She smiles at me, but looks away shyly, focusing on her food. Her cheeks are slightly flushed, the pulse in her neck faster than sitting and eating can account for. She feels this, whatever it is between us. The air between us is charged with it, has been the entire time we have been near each other during the journey. She is shyer now, attempting to maintain a distance. Perhaps it's because the danger has passed.

Now is my opportunity. I relish the moment we can be alone without any distractions, without the anxiety and stress of traveling in the dangerous desert. I know that it will take time to build trust between us, to draw her closer to me, but I can feel how quickly my own feelings are growing.

I want more, and I want it quickly.

It is difficult to restrain myself, to not at the very least reach out to hold her hand as I have seen other lovers do. I force myself to maintain the foot of space I have left for decorum between us, though I want to be so much closer to her. It's as if we were cut from the same cloth long ago, perhaps in a different lifetime. Only to be reunited now through a fated turn of events.

Perhaps that is silly. This intensity of emotion makes it feel so possible. But I hold onto my control.

The females eat quickly, Kate included. I give her a scanning glance. They all need to eat more, gain more weight. They also need epis to recover, to gain strength and adapt here. I frown, looking at the humans for symptoms of epis withdrawal. I do not think they have had any epis, ever, judging from their lack of stamina and their weakened appearance. After they are done eating, I rise to my feet.

"I will show you to your quarters," I tell them. There are rooms that are ready and waiting for visitors since the city receives so many. I can likely find them all rooms near each other.

The group rises and follows me out, obviously exhausted and ready to sleep. As expected, I am able to find a hall with mostly empty rooms, assigning them to each of the females.

"Thank you, Errol," Nina says, stepping into her room gratefully. "I could sleep for a week."

"Sleep well," I say.

Then I have only Nora and Kate left. I feel my anticipation grow. I am so close to being alone with Kate.

I open the next-to-last door in the hall, saying, "Nora, this room will be yo—"

"Is it okay if I sleep with you in your quarters?" Nora interrupts to say anxiously to Kate. "I don't think I can be alone here."

My movements go completely still. I have noticed Nora seems to be the weakest of the group, the one most scared and needing the most reassurance. Kate, of course, does not turn her down. She is too caring, taking her role as the leader to seriously.

"Yeah, sure," she agrees, smiling at the other woman. "No problem."

Nora immediately relaxes, the tension leaving her, even as my own tension rises. I understand Nora needs comfort, but I was so close to finally having a moment alone with Kate!

Ah well. This is not something I have any control over.

"These quarters are larger than the others," I say, taking them to a different room than I had intended. I open the door, allowing them to look inside. Nora nods, stepping in. Kate steps in as well, turning to me.

"Thank you, Errol," she says, meeting my eyes. "For everything."

I would do so much more for her if she would allow. I do not say that. I do not want to push her too fast, inadvertently scare her away. So I simply nod.

"I would like to speak to you. Alone. If possible," I murmur, stepping slightly closer. I need to be more direct now that I do not have the opportunity I thought I would.

She licks her lips, the movement drawing my eyes and reigniting my arousal. Not that I am ever completely calm in her presence.

"I—"

"Kate?" Nora calls out. "Is everything okay?"

Kate gives me an apologetic look, but it is also holds a hint of guilty relief.

"I'm sorry—I have to go."

"I understand." And I do. "Rest well."

Despite the mild words, I know my eyes are not at all calm and serene. I know they tell her I will be back for that talk.

She bites her lip, her eyes not leaving mine until she gently closes the door between us.

7

KATE

I squirm on the make-shift bed. The rustle of the well-worn cloth sounds incredibly loud in the quiet of the room. I go still, the softness nice under my body after spending days never fully reclining in the rover. It's much cooler than outside in the desert too. In short, I'm a lot more comfortable than I've been in days. I should have passed out already by now just because of that.

My eyes are still wide open, staring at the ceiling above as I struggle to settle in, and I know exactly why.

Errol's handsome face flashes across my mind, that determined glint in his eye that told me it wasn't over when I had to cut our talk short. I shiver a little at the memory. He's so incredibly sexy, big, like all the Zmaj but the coloring of his scales is different. Seven feet tall at least with that tail, you'd think wouldn't look good, but it only adds to his presence. The tips of his wings rise over his shoulders even when folded, and his voice is a deep, rumbling bass. All that combined with the care he's shown. The bravery and intelligence. I just can't seem to shake this attraction I have towards him.

With a sigh, I turn over to my side, and consider the problem. But then I immediately reconsider that word. Is it really a problem, this draw he has for me? Why do I want to think of it like that from the get go? Hmm.

What if...I pursue the attraction? Stop running and just...see what happens. Could there be more there than just the physical? Maybe the possibility of an emotional connection? And perhaps even more than that. Could love be an actual possibility here?

I frown, turning onto my stomach, trying to get comfortable. Though the bed isn't the problem right now, is it? I let out a huff of breath.

I've been operating in survival mode ever since we crashed on Tajss, just trying to live 'til the next day. That's what life has become and how I've pictured the future when I allow myself to think about it. But what if there is a chance at actual happiness on this planet? A reason to live beyond living itself here? Wouldn't that be a step up?

We'll never find a way off Tajss. If there had been a way, I'm betting Rosalind would have figured it out by now. We're years in at this point. However, maybe there is something else to hope for. Something that might actually be attainable.

I can almost feel that little seed of hope, the hope that finally pushed me out of the tunnels, growing at the thought. Now that I've seen this city, I have to resist the urge to beat myself up over not leaving even sooner. Not because they were so horrible to live in, but because the city suggests there might be more to find here on this planet, more to do than simply struggle to exist like Annabel would have us do.

Now that I'm away from her and the atmosphere she fostered, I can see even more clearly how much of a tyrant she has become. I'm surprised it took me this long to gather the wherewithal to leave. It just shows how much we'd all been beaten down by everything, doesn't it? But that doesn't matter now. There's no use re-hashing the past over and over. What's done is done. I close my eyes, determined to shut off my mind and sleep finally.

But that only has me thinking of Errol again. The intensity of his eyes, the chiseled musculature forged by hard work, the clean musk of his scent. And, just like Gomul, he's tall. Much taller than the average human, maybe around seven feet.

That's a lot of dragon-man for a petite woman like me, but there's no denying the electric charge of the air around us when we're together. The way my body aches to be touched by him. I can feel the echoes of it even now, just thinking of him. The situation is getting more desperate the more I'm around him. Thinking about him like this doesn't help, but it's like I have no control over my own brain when it comes to him.

He's the last thing on my mind as I finally drift off, my body too tired to stay awake despite my thoughts, Nora's steady breathing helping lull me into sleep.

Where my dreams take over. They're embarrassingly dominated by Errol, by his rippling muscles, his gorgeous face. In my own personal fantasy, he's actually touching me. And he isn't shy about it. I feel my heartbeat quicken, feel myself break out in a sweat as skin touches skin, his hands all over me as he moves in that—

I wake abruptly when the door to our room opens.

"Sorry," Nora says with a sheepish smile as she steps in. "I was just checking to see if any of the others were awake."

"No problem," I say, feeling oddly disoriented as I take a deep breath. I'm sweatier than the temperature calls for. And definitely a lot more slick in another place than I should be. Jeez. It's been a long time since I was a teenager. This really shouldn't be happening.

I sit up, swinging my legs over the side of the bed,

keeping my face down. I really hope that world-class wet dream doesn't show on my face, but I figure it's probably best not to give Nora a good look at it quite yet. I need to act normal. What would normal, not hot-and-bothered Kate say?

"How do you feel about breakfast?" I ask in a surprisingly even voice. Go me!

She brightens.

"That would be great!" she says eagerly. "I'm starving."

Good. Something else to focus on. And now that I've mentioned it, I could do with some food as well, so I haul myself out of bed to get ready.

By the time we dress and head out to the hall, most of the other women who arrived with me are also wandering out, looking better for the rest. They still don't look as good as the other survivors in this place. Maybe it's because the city people have more food and are exposed to less heat? Something still feels off about that. There's a vitality that's missing in our group, one that I see in the others here. Maybe we'll regain it if we spend a little time here. Only time will tell, in that case.

"Where are we going?" Nora asks, looking over at me expectantly as we start walking down the hall.

"I think we should just go to the same communal area Errol took us to yesterday. At least we know where it is."

Nobody can argue with that logic. So that's where we go. Since it's breakfast time, there's food already laid out and more people seated at the tables than when we first arrived yesterday.

We keep mostly to ourselves, though we try to chat a bit with those around us. The ship was big—some of the faces are familiar, but some of them have faded from memory. It feels a bit odd to be around so many people after being in such a small group for so long, but in a good way.

The low buzz of conversation stops, sudden silence falling across the room that's immediately filled with low, bubbling laughter.

"Tag!" a girlish voice yells.

Looking for the source a commotion at the far end of the room pulls my attention. A small person, no more than two feet tall, lands on the long dining table and runs down the middle, giggling loudly. She's wearing a soft pink shirt and a cloth diaper. Tiny scaled legs pump fast as she runs, arms flailing, knocking trays and glasses over as she passes.

"Rverre!" another female voice shouts, cutting across the outcries of those who are now wearing their breakfasts.

Behind the first small person runs another. This one is wearing no shirt and a pair of tan pants. Small horns sprout from his head, slightly curling back towards his ears, and shimmery scales cover his face and chest.

"I'll get you!" he cries, his voice cherubic.

"Illadon!" yet another female shouts. "Get down! Now!"

Neither of the small people are listening to the voices. The first one is closer to me now and I get my first good look. It's obviously a baby girl with a wide smile on her face and deeply blue tinted scales along her body. Brilliant green eyes sparkle with joy as she laughs. Tiny wings spread as she leaps into the air, gliding several feet down the table and lands in the middle of my plate. Food splatters up into my face and I throw myself back, trying to avoid the worst of it.

"Sorry," she says, barely pausing before she's running once more.

"Rverre, no fair, we said no wings!" the other cries, leaping also and landing a couple of feet behind her.

He's taller than her, his bare chest already showing the beginnings of the Zmaj physique. His scales show even more colors, sparkling blues, yellows, and greens mix along the edges. His eyes are green but have bright gold flecks that catch the light. His tiny tail swings back and forth.

He puts one foot in front of the other and is about to leap again, but as he does two massive arms snatch him out of the air right over my head.

Crouching down into my chair and swiveling my head to peer behind me, there's a full-grown Zmaj man who has grabbed the boy and is wrestling him to his chest. The coloring of his scales is similar to the young boy's and he has the same green eyes. It's more than obvious he's the boy's father.

"Illadon," the man says, voice soft. "Listen to your mother."

"Ah, dad," the boy whines.

"Illadon, you need to apologize, you know better than to run in the dining area," a woman says, huffing up next to the man.

The woman is lithe with long, brown hair that hangs past her shoulders and milky white skin that is too pure to be believed. She looks at the mess in front of me and her mouth drops open into an O.

"I'm so sorry," she says, pushing past me and scraping the mess onto a tray. "I'll get you another helping."

"It's fine," I say, unable to take my eyes off the boy.

She's his mother? He's the father? Can that be right? I must have heard something wrong.

The boy struggles in his father's grip but doesn't stand a chance. Another diminutive woman with almond shaped eyes walks up with the other child on her hip. The baby, if it's still such, is almost half her size, forcing her to walk with her hip cocked out to one side to offset the child's weight.

"Rverre, look what you've done," the new woman admonishes the child.

"I'm sorry," the child says, her voice cheery. "Hug?"

She holds her arms out towards me, tiny hands opening and closing.

"I'd... love a hug," I say, stumbling over my words in the moment of disbelief.

Children. Cross-children, inter-racial? Is that what you would call it? Inter-species?

Opening my arms, the child leaps into them and squeezes my neck hard. She's strong and adorable and too much. Tears form in the corners of my eyes, tears of joy, of relief, of hope. Squeezing her tightly back I hold on to her like she's the last rock before I go over a waterfall.

"You smell good," she says into my ear.

"Thank you," I say, letting her go reluctantly.

Tingling runs from my fingers up to my elbows. A baby. It's a real, talking, actual baby. It's not only a baby but there's no doubt that it's a mixed-race baby.

"You must be the new folks," the smaller woman says. "I'm Jolie."

She holds out one hand, cocking her hip to the side so Rverre rests easier. She's so small that I can't imagine how hard it must be to hold the baby and remain standing.

"Hi," I say, taking her hand. "I'm Kate."

She grins, an infectious smile that lights up her dark eyes and makes her face beam.

"So glad to meet you!" she exclaims, then jerks me into a rough, one-armed hug. Stepping back, she points at the other two. "This is Calista, Ladon, and that is Illadon."

"As in, World of Warcraft?" I ask, arching an eyebrow.

"Yeah," Calista laughs. "Hey, Rverre is named for Doctor Who."

"Oh, wow, I missed that," I laugh along with them. "So... you can... I mean..."

I stumble over the words. It seems delicate, but I have to

know. How did anyone guess that our two entirely different species could... well breed?

"Yeah," Calista grins. "Trust me, it's possible."

"Wow," is all I can say.

Jolie pipes in, "We need to check in on Mei."

"Yes," Calista nods agreement.

The mood shifts, becoming instantly somber.

"Is she okay?" I ask, sensing the concern.

"Yeah," Calista answers, but there's a hesitation to her voice. She exchanges a look with Jolie. "Zmaj babies are big, too big for a human woman honestly. The birthing is difficult and they take twelve months to gestate. The last three or four months you're on bedrest. Mei is having a difficult time, that's all."

Jolie nods but the two of them exchange a look that says there's more going on than they're saying. I let it go. I'm new here and it's none of my business.

"It was nice to meet you both," I say.

The mothers add their well wishes then they leave. Sitting down and finishing my meal, the light buzz of conversation flows around me filled with the excitement of possible futures. My own thoughts turn to Errol. Could that be my future too? Four months of bedrest sounds terrible but holding a baby, a mix of the two of us and damn if those babies weren't the cutest thing ever.

We finish our meals—which include a wider variety of produce than we've become used to—then we hear about a small marketplace in the city dome.

"It isn't like the one we had on the ship," the guy warns us as he leaves. "But it's nice to have at all."

"Let's go!" Lanie says as soon as she hears about it.

"Yeah, that could be cool," Fallon agrees. "Even if we can't actually get anything."

Everyone's on the same page, including me. We haven't

had any kind of shopping since the ship. It would be stupid to pass up the opportunity.

We clean up after ourselves and head out of the communal dining hall to the section of the city we're pointed towards. There are more people out and about now that it's morning, and the crowd starts to thicken even more as we near the marketplace.

As reported, it's small, with a row of open-air stalls bordering a corner of an open square, but it's still fun to look at the wares for sale. Bags, hats, knives. There's a lot to see and we take our time doing so. It's a bit of a shock. After seeing the same people, the same walls, over and over again for so long, everything looks interesting.

Studying a woven wide-brimmed hat, I'm about to ask the vendor if she'd be willing to barter for a knife when I hear a familiar voice. My heartbeat picks up immediately.

"Thank you, I could really use this right now..." another vendor responds to that deep voice.

Not turning my head, I look over at the stall next to me, searching. My eyes collide with laser-focused blue-green ones. My breath hitches as I lock eyes with Errol. The dream from last night comes crashing back to me and I feel my cheeks flush. The vendor is speaking to him, but his attention is clearly on me. How long has he been watching me stare at that hat?

As I watch, he says something to the vendor that I don't catch. I'm still too busy staring. Then he walks over, a heavy bag in one hand.

"Hello, Kate," he greets me in that distinctive voice. I suppress a shiver of reaction. "Did you sleep well?"

The question is innocent enough, but my thoughts aren't. I feel my blush deepen even more at the triggered memories of the dreams I enjoyed last night. None of them safe for public consumption.

"Uh, fine," I stammer, knowing I'm beet red. One of the major downsides of being a redhead. There's practically no way to downplay when I'm embarrassed.

All right, I need to redirect here. Fast.

"What are you up to this morning??" I ask.

"I rose with the suns and now I am up." He tilts his head to the side. "Have you eaten?"

His literalness has me blinking in confusion and it takes me a moment to switch gears at his question.

"Yes."

"Good."

There's an awkward pause while we both stare at each other. I don't know about him, but it's like the sight of him has all my mental gears grinding to a halt. I cast around for another topic, glancing away to gather my thoughts. Rosalind sweeps past just then, her eyes scanning the marketplace.

They land on me, and she waves with a smile as she changes her direction, coming over to us instead. The sight of her is like a slap in the face, waking me up. Do I really want to do this? Seek something more with Errol? I don't want to be judged or be subject to the rules here, be controlled by yet another person even if she is a vast improvement over Annabel. And that might be exactly what happens if I'm with Errol. Maybe I should rethink how openly I want to entertain this chemistry between us.

"Hello, Kate, Errol," Rosalind greets us. "How are you and your group doing?"

"We're fine, thank you," I return, my emotions in turmoil.

"Rosalind," Errol interjects. "Has the new batch of epis arrived?"

"Yes. That's actually why I was looking for you, Kate," she says, her eyes shifting to me. "I asked for the hunters to harvest more epis this time to accommodate your group as well."

"Epis?" I question. "What's that?"

Rosalind and Errol exchange glances. He takes up the explanation.

"It is a plant," he says. "One that helps the body adapt to the harsh conditions here. I do not know how you have survived this long without it—human bodies are not built to live in a place like Tajss." He gives me a scanning glance, though it is clearly not one meant to be flirtatious. It looks too assessing. "But even though you have survived, everyone in your group is thin, pale, weaker than you should be."

A plant that helps us adapt? Is this why everyone here looks so much healthier than we do?

"It sounds almost too good to be true," I say lightly, though my wariness is real. It sounds like some kind of drug.

Rosalind and Errol exchange another glance. There's something they aren't telling me. When Rosalind tacks on her portion, I know I'm right.

"There is a catch," she admits. "I want you to know all the facts before you take it, but I will say we all take it here, so that lets you know the benefits outweigh the risk." She takes a deep breath. "Once you take it, you are addicted to it. If you take it more than a handful of times, withdrawals could very well kill you. Even if you've only taken it once or twice, the withdrawals are no joke."

Errol nods as I listen with ever-widening eyes.

"The epis also needs to be fresh to impart the full benefit," he adds. "That is why the hunters here in the city make regular trips to harvest it from nearby zemlja caves, despite how dangerous an endeavor it is."

I shake my head.

"What are zemlja?" I ask, though there are many more questions running through my mind.

"They're giant wormlike creatures that spit acid. And yes, they're predatory," Rosalind answers with a grimace. "The epis only grows in their dens." She pauses. "I have to add, the epis also extends your lifespan along with giving you strength."

I feel completely overwhelmed. I cycle through the information dump quickly.

"Wait," I say. "So... that means we could never leave Tajss if we take it? It isn't a plant we can grow ourselves?"

"No," Errol says grudgingly. "You would be tied to Tajss."

"But it isn't like we're going anywhere, not realistically," Rosalind points out. "Even if we figured out the ship problem..."

She doesn't have to finish that thought. Even if we had a working ship, only our group hadn't taken the epis. We'd be resigning ourselves to dying en-route to our original destination rather than simply staying on Tajss. Perhaps another opportunity would present itself. But the chances of that are extremely slim if not non-existent.

"This is a lot to take in," I finally say. "Can I think about it?"

"Of course," Rosalind agrees. "But the fresher it is the better. And it just arrived. You will have to wait a while for the next shipment if you take too long."

Great. A time crunch on top of everything.

"I need to speak to my friends," I murmur to myself.

Rosalind nods briskly, stepping back.

"You do that. Everyone who wants a dose should come out to meet near the marketplace as soon as you decide."

"All right," I agree as she leaves.

That's a lot to pass on.

"Kate?"

I turn back at Errol's concerned voice, forcing a smile.

75

"I better head back to my group," I say, taking a step back. "It was good to see you."

"You should take the epis," he urges. "Otherwise, I fear your lifespans will be quite short."

"I'll take that into consideration."

He doesn't say anything more when I turn on my heel and push through the crowd. Running away from him as much as hurrying to talk to my group. I need time to think, to consider all the repercussions. Both for Errol and for epis. Though, currently, one is much more important.

I rejoin the other women, the lightheartedness of the shopping trip obliterated as I fill them in.

"Wait—there's a magical plant that will fix how shitty we feel here?" Fallon asks. "Sign me up!"

"It likely changes us on a cellular level, adjusts our DNA," Lanie mutters to herself.

"Is that good or bad?" I ask.

She shrugs.

"Everyone here seems to be fine. And we're not exactly thriving, from a health standpoint." She pauses, nodding to herself. "I'm in. I want to feel good for whatever life we're able to build here."

In the end, there isn't a whole lot of debate about our decision. Not when we can literally see how much better everyone in the city is doing. We go down to the meeting point, where Rosalind is already waiting with the plant.

Errol is there as well, his shoulders relaxing as he sees us arrive. But he doesn't try to come closer, simply watches from a short distance away while he speaks to another Zmaj. I can feel the weight of his gaze as Rosalind presents a dose of the plant to each of us.

"How often do we need to take this?" Lanie asks as she takes the plant.

"Once a week in the beginning, for about a year. Then it

should taper off to a maintenance dose a few times a year, to avoid withdrawals," she responds.

"And we just...eat it?" Nora asks dubiously.

"Yes. It doesn't taste bad."

I stare down at the light blue, glowing plant.

"Here goes nothing," I mutter, bringing it up to my mouth.

The others watch me do it. Then they look at each other and follow suit, one by one.

When I bite down, a cooling sensation immediately sweeps through me. It has a spicy mint flavor that rushes through my body. The change is immediate. The slight headache I've been living with for the most of our time here disappears, the touch of nausea, the digestive discomfort...all of it leaves. And I'm not hot. In fact, I feel cool.

The others must be feeling something similar because when I look at their faces, they appear just as shocked as I am.

"Wow," Ashlee breathes. "I feel like a person again!"

That exclamation draws unanimous agreement from all of us. That's exactly what it feels like. We've been functioning at a fraction of our energy for so long that we didn't even really remember what it felt like to feel good.

But even as I wonder at the change, I can't get my mind off Errol. I can feel his eyes on me as we move away, leaving to get lunch. I don't look at him, feeling too vulnerable in that moment, too physically off-kilter to also throw in the complication of him. But I'm still thinking of him through lunch. And all the way to the small celebration Rosalind and her mate throw that night.

She invited everyone in the city but also those of Errol's tribe, so the party is actually pretty big, with different personalities mixing. I try to have a good time as I speak with humans and Zmaj alike. I'm intrigued by how intermixed everything is, how natural and cohesive it all feels. Though maybe I shouldn't be. Even our group ended up living with a Zmaj to survive, didn't we? We're lucky they were here to help all of us.

"This is pretty rare," Sarah explains as the celebration goes on around us. "A carefree party isn't usually high on the priority list."

I nod. It makes sense and falls in line with Rosalind's leadership style. I would never peg her as the celebrating-for-celebration's-sake type. I see a couple of our group dancing and others drinking some of the homemade alcohol. Everyone's having a good time it seems. Except me. I'm too preoccupied to really let loose.

My eyes inevitably find Errol again. It's like I can't focus on anything else when he's in the vicinity. He nodded at me when I arrived and I nodded back. But that was it.

There's a weirdness between us now, an uncomfortable tension that wasn't there before. One that I regret. Maybe I should—

A Zmaj with red scales steps into my line of sight, an open smile on his face.

"Would you like some of the zeeker we've brewed?" he asks, holding out a full cup.

I smile back automatically, taking the cup to be polite. He's trying to be friendly, which I appreciate. Even if I'm not even remotely in the mood.

"Thank you," I say.

"You are quite welcome. I hear..."

As he continues the conversation, I listen with half an ear as my eye is drawn back to where I saw Errol last, only to see the back of him as he pushes through the crowd, out towards the edge. Where is he going? Once he pushes through the crowd, he quickly disappears into an alley. Leaving the party completely.

8

ERROL

"*E*rrol! Where are you going? The festivities have only just begun!"

I nod at Drosdan, but I don't answer his questions, not even smiling back as I continue on my way. I can see the confusion on his face, but I cannot pretend to be in a good mood despite the revelry around us.

After seeing Kate at the celebration, I am much thornier than usual. It is as though I am experiencing a micro-bijass towards my own kind, one that raises those haunting memories I came to the city to leave behind. Memories of the animalistic state I fell into after our society crumbled. That period in which I lost all sense of self to violence and an utter emptiness. But I suppose it is no wonder that running from oneself is not possible.

I push the memories away again with a focused effort, though I feel them still lurking in the back of my mind, ready to reemerge at the slightest sign of weakness. I know I am withdrawing into myself because of these ugly feelings, these unwelcome memories, but I do not know how else to process my emotions, not when they are so strong, so utterly volatile.

And I know exactly what the trigger was. I feel very possessive over Kate, have felt so since I first saw her, before I even knew her as a person. Seeing her speaking with other Zmaj males at the event, accepting drink from them-- I deliberately unclench my fists, cutting off the growl that emerged unbidden. It does not matter how I feel about her speaking to other males. She has not given herself to me. Not only that, she has pulled back from me several times over these past few days, a clear indication she does not want to pursue what is between us. My poor internal reaction to that is not something I am proud of—in fact, I feel ashamed of it. That shame reminds me of my intention to live this new chance at life with as much peace as can be had.

I cannot continue on this way if peace is my goal. I do not want to risk my well-being, my internal equilibrium. I sigh to myself. The decision is a difficult one to make, but one that I think is best. I need to establish some distance from Kate despite this unprecedented attraction I feel for her. If she does not want me, torturing myself by being close to her does not make any rational sense. And I need to be reasonable and rational now, more than ever.

But as soon as I decide that logic should prevail, Kate's image appears in my mind. And her scent haunts my senses. Despite my newfound resolve, it wears on my normally fierce will. Growling under my breath, I push aside the memory of her as firmly as I set aside the others.

Kate is dangerous for me, for my well-being. She raises territorial feelings that are better left untouched, because those feelings are strong enough to wake something deep inside me—something I want to stay safely asleep. Leaving the celebration is a good decision. If I must watch Kate interact with more Zmaj males while deliberately staying away from me...

My snarl is quiet, and nobody is nearby to hear it, but I still feel shame again at my loss of control. Yes, leaving is a good decision.

Simply knowing it was a good decision doesn't make me calm when I reach my quarters. It takes some time for the aggression to fade. Thoughts of what Kate might be doing at the party keep invading my mind. Eventually, I do fall into a fitful sleep late into the night. Not that the rest is particularly restful.

I do not feel much happier when I wake the next day, and Rosalind calls me into a private meeting.

"Thank you for coming, Errol," she greets from behind her desk.

"Of course," I respond, taking a seat in one of the chairs across from her. I do not know why she called me in, but she is the clear leader here in the dome. Accepting such invitations is a good idea to keep relations on good terms. Fortunately, she does not keep me waiting long.

"I have a favor to ask of you," she says baldly.

"What is it?" I ask. I already brought the order she asked for. What else can I contribute that she desires?

"You were the first of us Kate and her group encountered. And the person they've spent the most time with since." She leans forward. "I would really appreciate it if you can find out some information for me."

"What kind of information?" I ask, though I think I have a good idea what she wants. I find it better to have things spelled out so there is no confusion.

"I want to know how they survived for this long," she responds bluntly. I appreciate the candor. "Who helped? Because both you and I know they aren't alive without help from outside sources." That is true. I had thought exactly the same thing. "I want to be sure there aren't any dangers coming from this new direction. If we don't have the information, we can't anticipate or plan for whatever the threat might be in order to better protect ourselves."

I understand. That is a good reason and another clear example of why she is a good fit for her position.

"I do not sense any danger," I say carefully. "I feel as though Kate is simply reserved because she does not know what to expect here. And does not know how far she can trust any of us."

Me included, and that may not change now. I let that thought and the pain of it drift away. I cannot dwell upon it. It is not something I have control over.

Rosalind nods.

"I trust you and your judgment, Errol. I really do."

"But?" I ask.

She smiles at me.

"I would still appreciate if you could find out all you can."

That is fair. But Kate has pulled back from me, withdrawn for a reason or reasons I do not fully understand. Perhaps a different approach would be more fruitful.

"I will encourage Kate to talk to you herself," I decide. "I am certain she will anyway, with time."

"Hmm." Her sharp eyes scan me as she relaxes somewhat, leaning back in her chair and dropping the commanding posture she so often dons. I do not think she even does it consciously. "I trust you'll do the right thing, Errol. You always do."

I incline my head.

"I hope I will not disappoint," I say, standing at the clear dismissal.

"You won't," she says with a toothy smile. "Oh, and I wanted to invite you to dinner tonight as well. You will come, won't you?"

"Of course. Thank you for your invitation."

She nods, saying goodbye as I turn to leave the room.

I think nothing of the invitation apart from the fact that I will now have to stay in the city until tomorrow, at the very least. That is, I think nothing of it until I arrive for the dinner. I did not realize I was not the only one she invited to the meal.

Kate appears just as surprised to see me as I am to see her when I arrive, but we each express polite greetings and sit down to eat.

It is only dinner.

After we eat, we can both go our separate ways. Perhaps this is Rosalind's attempt to increase Kate's comfort with me, to make it more possible that she will tell me the information Rosalind wants. If she had asked me, I could have let her know the effort would be wasted. I deliberately keep my eyes on my food. I simply must get through this dinner.

"...and I know that your rover is still sitting out in the desert, unprotected."

"Yes," Kate agrees. "But I can't move it until it's fixed."

I look up to see Rosalind nodding.

"I believe I have the tools you need to get it running again, you're welcome to borrow them."

Kate visibly brightens at the news.

"That would be great!" she gushes. "Thanks, Rosalind. I really appreciate it. And I know the others will too."

Despite myself, I cannot tear my gaze away from her. From her bright beauty, the glow shining from inside her at the good news.

But it is not just the news, is it? The epis has restored a vitality she was missing before, enhancing her natural beauty. Her eyes are clearer, her hair shines brighter, her skin almost glows. If I am not mistaken, she has already gained some weight as well, weight that she needed on her slender frame. And it is also clear she has much more energy than before.

Even as I stare, I admonish myself for doing so. How can I maintain my distance when I cannot even comply with my own resolution not to stare at her?

"Perhaps Errol can join you on your trip."

What? That jolts me out of my own internal dialogue. I finally look away from Kate to meet Rosalind's eyes.

"Are you available Errol?" she prods, her eyes urging me to agree. "I am certain Kate would very much appreciate your company and protection to retrieve her vehicle."

I know what she is doing. She wants me to extract the information she wants from Kate. I should not say yes. This is the exact opposite of maintaining my distance. I will go mad being so close while being unable to touch, unable to explore that electricity between us.

"Oh, I don't need—" Kate starts, her expression turning alarmed.

But I cut in before she can refuse me, adopting a dutiful face to mask my true emotions. "I'd be glad to help."

Because I am weak. I cannot ignore the yearning in my heart despite my best efforts. How can I resist a chance to be alone with her, spend real time in her presence?

Kate nods at my acceptance, looking down at her meal. "I —thank you," she murmurs.

"It is no trouble." It is, in fact, unavoidable, at least for me.

The rest of the meal is more subdued, though Rosalind attempts to keep the conversation light and carefree after achieving her goal. She is a master at manipulation, trapping the both of us in the very scenario that she thinks will do the most good. That will accomplish the outcome she desires.

I cannot fault her for it. Her intentions are to protect

everyone she feels responsible for, even if it might mean discomfort for some.

Still, I do not linger after we finish the meal. I fear I may give too much away if I speak to Kate privately. I might reveal how much my desire for her is tearing me apart inside.

9

KATE

I adjust the pack on my back as I take another step forward. Even after just that short stay in the city dome, I'd almost forgotten how searing the suns are out here in the open, how oppressive the heat without any shade to cut it.

On the other hand, it still doesn't feel nearly as horrible as it did on the way into the city. The only thing that's different is that I had the epis. I have a new lease on life. Nothing hurts, the heat is still oppressive but immensely more bearable. I feel like my muscles and bones are stronger, my head clearer. I didn't realize how terrible I was feeling until I just...didn't.

I flick a glance over at Errol. If only the physical discomfort hadn't been supplanted by this quiet tension between Errol and me. He's maintained his position a little ahead and to the side of me the entire time we've been traveling, his sharp gaze constantly scanning the horizon, watching for threats. He's been silent apart from when it is absolutely necessary to speak. Keeping his distance both literally and figuratively.

I look away again. It's a sad change from our first trip together, when he'd been attempting to make conversation. Trying to get closer instead of further away. It's like he's decided to build a wall between us, a solid one. I don't completely blame him for it. I tried to create the distance first, didn't I?

I frown as I take another step forward. This is what I wanted. Some separation between us, a way to quiet the attraction, the uncomfortable feelings he engenders in me. But if this is really what I wanted, why does it feel so terrible? Why do I feel like I lost something precious, something important?

I miss the more open Errol, the Errol that didn't hide his interest. He's been strange around me, especially after Rosalind's party when he saw that other Zmaj speaking to me. And I find I don't like it. Not at all. Now that I've had a taste of that electric energy that's possible between us, I'm almost...addicted to it. I crave it. Even though it's given me fitful, hot nights in the city.

I've never felt like this before—not even close. Never yearned for a man like this, wanted one so badly I couldn't shake the feeling despite my best intentions.

Right from the very beginning, Errol started this thirst in me that only he could quench.

He's different. Not just because he's Zmaj. That doesn't really factor into it all, really. It's who he is. Somehow, he speaks to the core of me, who I am deep inside, the parts that nobody really knows. That connection has kicked off a storm I'm not sure I can contain for much longer, despite my resolve, my decision to protect myself from this *thing*.

This is an aspect of myself I've never touched before, and it sure isn't comfortable to deal with it now. I've always been an observer, looking in from a distance. Careful, slow to act. Considering all the possibilities and all the repercussions and making the logical choice. And sticking to that choice, often with an iron-clad resolve. But that doesn't seem to be working in this case, no matter how hard I try to regulate my emotions.

There's an urgency here, a sense of time running out that I just can't ignore. If I let Errol withdraw too much for too long, I could miss my chance to grab onto this feeling between us, build something worthwhile with it. I feel that push inside me, that gut feeling that wants me to tell him he isn't crazy. That I'm drawn to him just as strongly as he is to me, that I want him too. Want him just as badly, if not even more than he does. I have the urge to say that I made a mistake. That I regret it.

Frustration beats at me. Why should I care about Rosalind's judgment, or anyone else's for that matter? I've been observing while in the city, both how people interact day to day and at the gatherings. There are plenty of couples in the city, even babies for God's sake! I was being completely irrational, grasping at any excuse to hide behind so I wouldn't have to deal with this frighteningly strong attraction between us.

We're not on the ship anymore, haven't been for years. The same rules no longer apply. I need to get out of that headspace, stop acting like ship protocol matters at all. I mean, there isn't even a ship! That should have been the first giant clue here. I shake my head at myself. Just shows how ingrained it was in us, how difficult a habit it is to break when that's how we lived our entire lives before wrecking on this planet.

All right.

Okay.

If I regret the distance, then I need to do something about it. Easier said than done, but then, isn't that true of anything worthwhile? I take a deep breath, wondering how I can break this uneasy silence. In the end, I can't think of any natural way, so I just go for it.

"How much farther is it?" I ask, immediately smacking myself mentally. What a great conversation starter. Not at all annoying.

"Not long," he replies after a beat of silence, not even turning to look at me. Wonderful.

Well, I've never been a quitter and I don't plan on starting now.

"Uh...do you plan to stay in the city for long?"

I know it isn't his actual home.

"No," he replies.

I wait a beat to see if he'll expand on that. Surprise, surprise. He doesn't. Great. I'm making absolutely no headway. I fall silent again, wondering how I can pull Errol back out of internal hiding. Or if I can at all. He's closed himself off from me completely. There may as well be a giant blinking arrow above his head with a sign saying, "Closed to Kate".

I don't like it. How did we end up here after that initial explosive attraction between us? I don't know. Maybe it's already too late. I bite my lip, hoping that isn't the case, worrying at the problem as we continue to traverse the desert.

Errol was right about the distance left—it doesn't take us much longer to reach the rover, still sitting exactly where we left it. Although that isn't a shocker. It isn't like it can be driven away in its current state, even if someone happened across it out here. I give it a quick once-over in case other animals may have been drawn to it while it sat there, a giant dark interruption in the rolling red sand. it's still shut tight, unscathed. Well, as unscathed as it was when we left it.

I move over to the hood after I look it over and lift it up.

Errol follows, setting down the pack with the tools next to me. I lean into the engine, orienting myself.

"Would you mind giving me the pliers?" I ask. Then realize I don't know what they would call them here. "The tool that can grip—"

"This one?" He hands me the sturdy-looking tool.

"Yes," I say, taking it. "Thank you." I get to work with the pliers and the scissors I have in my pocket.

"What are you doing?" Errol asks, his eyes interested as he watches.

"Trying to get the worst of the scorched area cleared away so I can see what I'm doing," I explain, removing pieces of the metal and plastic.

"Ah." A beat of silence. "Would you like some help?"

"Sure," I agree, surprised at his desire to work alongside me. "Here, you can use the knife..."

He gets to work with me, taking direction easily. He's a quick study and defers to me as we work together, no ego in sight. It just makes me admire him more and wish for something else at the same time.

When it comes time to weld, he hands me the appropriate tools and steadies the parts for me as I work carefully.

"Don't move," I order as I melt the metallic pieces together. "If I make a mistake, this will be a much longer fix. We might have to go back to the city and rummage for parts."

"I understand," he murmurs, his voice rock steady, just as his hands are. I couldn't ask for a better helper.

I finish patching the engine up, hoping this will do it. It takes some time because I'm extremely careful, moving slowly. Better to fix it once correctly than have to fix the repairs later. That's always been my motto and it's saved me a lot of time in the past when others were rushing around me.

Errol helps me patiently, not complaining once as he watches me work. Finally, I straighten, pushing at the small of my back. I've been bent over so long that it's sore from the position.

"It is done?" Errol asks watching me.

I shrug, staring down at the seams I've created.

"Hope so," I say. "Let me try to start it. That's the only way to know for certain." I open the driver's side and sit down. Moment of truth. Come on. Don't let me down. I close my eyes and push the button, praying it'll work.

The rover immediately responds, turning on, the display coming to life in front of me.

"It is working?" Errol asks, his tone excited.

I jump out of the still open door, thrusting my fists into the air in victory.

"Yes!" I cry out. "It's fixed!"

Errol grins at my antics, the ice breaking in that moment of celebration. I punch him in the shoulder, so excited to have resurrected the rover.

"No small thanks to you, Errol! I wouldn't have—"

My gratitude is cut short as Errol hooks his arm around my waist and pulls me into his body. I get a flash of his intense eyes.

His lips are on mine, soft and sure and just...

Perfect.

Oh.

My surprise gives way quickly to passion as my arms come up to wrap around his neck, meeting him caress for caress. As his taste, the feel of him, his scent all hit me, I wonder why I was ever fighting this. What kind of idiot would say no to Errol? Not me. Not anymore.

More. What I need is more. I press harder against the front of him, feeling exactly how excited he is. Oh, man. That's...a lot of man.

But Errol breaks the kiss, frowning. Panting, I start to ask what's wrong when his eyes widen.

"Into the rover. Quickly!"

I don't ask questions. The urgency in his tone is enough to get me moving instantly, just as the sand flies up from the ground just yards away as the first meteorite hits.

I cry out as hot sand spatters against us, trying to shield my eyes from the assault. Errol's hand closes around mine and he pulls me the rest of the way to the rover, shoving me inside. He follows the next instant with all our tools and gear in his hands. As soon as he's inside, a meteorite hits the roof above us, the impact loud enough that it leaves my ears ringing.

"There is cover in that direction," Errol shouts, pointing. "We should take shelter there."

Copy that. The rover is still on, so I press the accelerator and head over in the direction he indicates, trying to calm my heart after that double shot of adrenaline. The rover is armored, but I don't want to test that with a meteorite shower.

We're hit multiple times as we drive, the sand in front of us exploding with more hitting the ground. There's no way to avoid them, so I don't try. Just try to drive as quickly as I can to minimize the amount of time we spend out in the open.

"There!"

I follow Errol's finger to a rock formation, one that has a thick ledge covering a shallow space underneath. Not perfect, but better than being out here with nothing. Turning the wheel hard, I slide the rover into that shallow space, making the most of it. Errol gasps at the skidding move, staring at the vertical stone less than a foot away from his side of the vehicle when we rock to a stop.

"I have a lot of practice," I say mildly, trying not to laugh at his horrified expression.

"Uh...yes." He clears his throat, relaxing the tight knuckled grip he has on the door. "I can see that."

I bite my lip and look away, giving both him and me time to compose ourselves for completely different reasons. When I look up, I see I have most of the rover under the ledge. It's the best I can do with this space.

On the other side of my window, the burning rocks keep on slamming into the ground. The reverberation of the impact travels through the ground and up into the rover. The power the meteorites hit the land with is no joke.

"How long will it last?" I ask, fascinated at the sight. If it weren't so dangerous, it would be beautiful.

"I do not know," Errol replies. "We will see."

So we sit and wait it out. A few minutes in, Errol reaches out for my hand. I don't even need to think about it before I lay my hand in his, noting how small and delicate mine looks in his large and sturdy one. That's a first for me. He closes his fingers, and now his dry, warm palm comforts me as the flaming rocks hit Tajss.

For hours.

The rover's metal is sturdy, but without the ledge above us, I doubt it would have been able to withstand the amount of battering. We were lucky we had the rover. Lucky that there was also cover nearby. This could have been so much worse.

We don't really talk as we wait, the sound of the storm loud enough that we have to raise our voices to be heard. So we simply sit. I don't mind, not now that the ice between us has broken. After a few hours, the storm finally stops—or at least pauses for a while.

Errol cranes his neck to look outside, squinting at the sky.

"There are more coming," he says. I look up as well and see

the bright spots of color barreling towards the ground in the distance. "The storm will likely continue for hours still. But we have time to leave the rover and settle in on the other side of the rock. The space there is not big enough for the rover, but it will cover us well and we will be able to sleep more comfortably."

I nod. That makes sense. I'm already feeling cramped in here, now that he's mentioned it. We grab some rations and blankets that were left in the rover since they were too much to carry. Then we hurry over to the other side of the rock formation.

The ledge on this side is lower, the space underneath deeper. He's right: It isn't big enough for the rover, but it's more than adequate for us. Errol goes in first, doing a sweep to make sure there aren't any animals lurking in the shadows. Then we set up a nest of blankets a good way under the cover to make sure we're protected from the meteorites and the hot sand they spray when they hit.

That taken care of, we sit down to eat. The traveling all day, the concentration it took to fix the rover, and then this excitement over the meteorite shower has really taken its toll on me. It must have for Errol as well because neither of us says much as we eat, though we can now.

After we both finish, he lies down in the soft nest and holds his arms out to me.

"Come, Kate," he murmurs. "I will keep you safe this night."

How can I refuse? Lying down with my back to his chest, I snuggle in as he wraps his strong arms around me, tucking his body protectively around my own. I should feel more scared out here in the relative open after encountering the things I have, but I don't. I relax, feeling safe, knowing Errol is there.

My eyes start to drift shut as I imagine what it would be like to sleep like this every night, in Errol's caring hold. I imagine myself traveling to his caves with him as his lover. I know I don't want to fight this anymore. So those possibilities don't only seem like fantasies anymore. They feel possible. Images of Errol and the future we can make together swirl through my head as sleep slowly claims me, a smile lingering on my face.

10

ERROL

J wake before Kate does. It is no hardship. I press my lips against the softness of her hair, her warm body lax and trusting against mine, her face soft in sleep. I move a lock of shining hair away from her cheek.

She is so beautiful. Capable, too. I never expected to feel arousal stirring just from watching her work on the rover. But I did. Watching her capable hands work on the alien technology, her confidence in her skill... I feel myself stirring simply thinking of it again.

The kiss had been impulsive, an unthinking act that occurred as a culmination of so many moments I'd held myself back, tried to maintain control, afraid to be rejected. When I finally had Kate in my arms, her lips under mine, I worried that my fear was well-founded. In my mind's eye, I saw her rejecting me, and then I would shatter like a piece of meteorite glass. But she didn't.

When her lips moved, when she leaned into the caress, I felt a rush of relief. And then my arousal increased tenfold, before the meteorite shower interrupted us.

I lay my hand on Kate's hip. This is not at all what I

expected to happen on this trip. I accepted the escort request because I could not turn down the opportunity to spend time with Kate, despite my resolve to maintain my distance. I was confident that I could control myself, that my reservations would help me make the wise choice. I thought I would be able to spend time with her but not venture closer in any meaningful way, any dangerous way that would leave me vulnerable to further hurt.

I shake my head ruefully. Those thoughts sound so ridiculous to me now. There is no such thing as control for me, not around Kate. She is my weakness. I am already vulnerable. What is the point of keeping my distance now?

The fact that I thought I could escort her to her vehicle, help her when she needed it, but otherwise keep myself away from her was a clear example of the delusional thinking I fostered simply to have what I wanted. But I do not blame myself. I would have told myself anything, justified this trip in any way I could have to spend more time with Kate.

She starts to stir in my arms, her eyes fluttering open. She smiles when she sees me, filling my heart with warmth.

"Good morning," she murmurs.

I smile back, combing my fingers through strands of her silky hair.

"Yes, it is," I return.

Her smile widens, her cheeks turning adorably pink as she sits up gracefully.

"Are you hungry?" she asks, reaching for the food. "Because I'm starving."

"I am hungry," I say gently, allowing her to change the subject. I am no longer uncertain about her attraction to me, not after the way she kissed me back yesterday. I can be patient, move forward as slowly as she needs. I watch her arrange the food, enjoying the intimacy of waking up with her, having breakfast together. This is nice. And the food is quite good, better than expected. We eat the smoked meat and fruits in companionable silence, the early morning light not as harsh as it will become as the day continues.

I am glad she has an appetite now, the epis no doubt increasing her hunger. I will be happy to see her gain even more weight on her slender frame. I frown as I continue to chew, feeling something tickle the back of my brain. There is something oddly familiar about this food, something that wakes up those memories I keep attempting to suppress. I shake my head, pushing them away again. It is simply food. That is it.

"Here, this is delicious," Kate says, offering me some more dried fruit.

"Thank you," I say, my fingers brushing hers as I take the offering. Even that small touch sends a tingle through me. Her eyes meet mine for a searing moment, but then she looks away again, biting her lip. I feel my hearts start to beat faster, my body start to quicken. I feel more raw emotion, more passion around Kate than I'm sure I can take.

My attention is focused on her as we continue to eat. There is nowhere else it could stray, not with her in front of me. Her leg brushing against mine. Our hands touching when we reach for the same piece of meat. The small touches are maddening, the tension between us building with each one of the inadvertent touches, with the closeness. I attempt to redirect my attention to maintain some semblance of propriety, though I fear it is a foregone conclusion that I will fail.

"Who cared for you and the other females?" I ask. Kate stills at the question, obviously not expecting it. "Who helped you procure this meat?"

I know there must be a Zmaj involved. They could not have survived this long alone, not with all the unfamiliar dangers here on Tajss, the difficulty in finding food, water, shelter. I have seen the difficulty the other humans had. I need to know. This is a question that has been more and more on my mind. I ask now for myself, not because Rosalind would like the information.

Did Kate take this Zmaj as a lover? Is that why she will not divulge his name? Jealousy is an ugly emotion, but I cannot deny it rears its ugly head as I fervently hope that is not the case.

Kate is silent for a long moment, until I wonder if she will again refuse to answer the question. But she does not refuse. She raises her eyes to meet mine.

"It was another Zmaj," she confesses. "An elder called Gomul."

I stare, my mind emptying completely. Gomul? I feel both hot and cold at once.

Kate watches me with concern, drawing closer. She places her hand on my arm, searching my face when I don't say anything.

"What is it, Errol?" she asks. "What's wrong?"

I blink, feeling tears prick my eyes.

"Gomul?" I clear my throat. "What does he look like?"

Frowning, she describes him. The color of his scales, his eyes... It would be too great a coincidence, especially in this area. But it is not possible. Is it?

"Errol, you're scaring me," Kate says, rubbing my forearm. "What is it?"

I meet her eyes, my vision blurring as the past rushes out of the gray mist of the bijass.

"Gomul is my father," I say, my throat tight and voice hoarse. "I thought he was gone. I didn't know he survived the Devastation." I cup her face and rub her lips with my thumb. "Thank you, Kate. I may have gone forever without knowing."

Leaning down, I kiss her softly. I fully believe now that

destiny brought us together. The chances of meeting Kate in the desert because I decided to go to the city when I didn't need to were already so slim.

Now, this news that my very own father, who I thought was lost forever, is the reason why Kate is alive today? These are not simple coincidences. We were meant to meet. Meant to be important to one another.

I slide my hands down her back, pulling her more tightly into my body. Her lips are gentle against mine, soft and clinging as she wraps her own arms around me. Giving. Offering comfort and gentleness in a world where both are often difficult to find.

Passion slowly rises, the softness giving way to more urgency as our bodies wake. Desire that can no longer be denied overtakes us. I do not want to deny it. I do not want to fight it.

Destiny has corded our fates, has brought us to this moment. We are meant to be with each other. My hearts beat quickly, my hands smoothing over Kate's body as my prime cock hardens fully. Wanting more. Wanting everything.

Kate breaks the kiss and stares into my eyes, her cheeks are a soft pink, and it is no longer because of embarrassment. Eyes full of the same heat I feel, she sits back, moving away from me. Her eyes lock with mine as her hands go to her clothes.

My breathing hitches as she disrobes leisurely, taking her time to reveal her smooth, pale skin. I've seen the human females, of course, but never without their protective clothing. Often, I've wondered at the soft mounds under their shirts, but I had no idea. The swell of flesh is beautiful, curving out and forming sweet mounds topped with pale pink tips. It's unlike anything I could have imagined. It's obvious they're intended for reproductive purposes but a Zmaj female has protective plates that cover and hide theirs.

Kate's are open, pressing out to the world, proudly pronouncing her femaleness.

My cock throbs looking at them and my mouth waters as I take in the dip of her waist, the roundness of her hips. The long length of her slim legs. She undoes her pants, slowly lowering them, sliding them down to reveal more soft skin. No scales, no protection. She needs none, I am her protector. Nothing will harm her perfection while I draw breath.

My eyes are drawn to the place where her legs meet and the soft fur there. The sunlight reflects off a hint of moisture and for some reason this makes my cock jump with excitement. I want, desperately, to bury myself in her most intimate place. Groaning, I reach and draw her back in as the last article of clothing falls, unable to resist touching her. My hands slide over her smooth warmth, wanting to touch her everywhere at once, my mouth again on hers. She is so sweet, so addicting. If she was my weakness before, I know it will only be worse after this, but I do not care.

I carefully lay her back against the blankets, my hands cupping the soft weight of her chest, sliding down her silky side, cupping the warmth that beckons me between her thighs. She gasps, spreading her legs farther apart to give me more room, her hand kneading the back of my neck, her hips thrusting up, asking for more. She need not ask.

As she moans I leave her mouth and kiss my way down her graceful neck. Down to the softness of her curves, to the hard points on top of her mounds and I take one into my mouth, sucking on it as she sinks her fingers into my hair, her moans making my cock throb harder. I let go of the reddened, wet peak to give the other one the same attention. When her legs are moving impatiently underneath me, I move even lower, skimming kisses down her flat stomach, pausing to nuzzle at the small indention at the base of her stomach.

My hands slide down to grip her inner thighs, spreading her farther apart, making room for my head. I want to taste her everywhere. She cries out sharply as I lick at her, drawing the flat of my tongue through her slick folds. The taste of her is intoxicating. My mind explodes with pleasure as I lap up her wetness with my tongue, driving it deeper into her. When I graze a small point at the top of her opening, she stiffens.

"Yes!" she cries out.

Focusing my attention on this special place I hold her down with a firm grip as she bucks against me and keep flicking my tongue against it.

Her body tenses. I redouble my efforts, sensing she is nearing her end. I moan as she jerks against me, a muffled scream signaling her pleasure. I keep my face against her until she goes limp again.

Panting, I sit up and take off my clothes, my eyes scanning her flushed body, the light layer of sweat that covers her. She is so perfect it's an almost physical pain. My need for her aches, my pleasure looking at her is overwhelming.

She opens her eyes, her lips slightly parting, roaming over my now naked body. When they reach my cock, her eyes widen and she rises onto her elbows. Her mouth drops open into an O.

"Oh," she exhales, not taking her eyes off my stiff member that hangs between us.

"Is something wrong?" I ask.

She shakes her head negative but doesn't lie down again. She sits up the rest of the way and one hand reaches for my cock. She runs her fingers down it, a light touch that causes a shiver down my spine.

"It's... ribbed," she says, giggling. "And big!"

Looking down then at her I try to understand what she's saying.

"Do your men not? Are they… smaller?" I ask, struggling to find the right word.

"Oh yeah," she says, moving her head closer to my prime cock.

Her tongue darts out and licks her lips then she licks the length of my shaft. Pleasure explodes, my eyes close and I throw my head back. I've never felt anything like this before. Overwhelming, intense, amazing. Her fingers trail along the sides, following her tongue as she moves up and down.

"We have to be careful," she says, her voice hoarse. "I want you but…"

She trails off. Lowering myself to my knees in front of her I nod, thoughtful.

"Of course," I answer, leaning in and pressing my lips to hers.

She lies onto her back again and spreads her legs, her eyes beckoning me in. Moving myself over her, my cock at her opening, I press my lips against hers.

"Errol…" she murmurs.

I kiss her sweet mouth as my primary cock nudges against her wet entrance. She is ready, but the fit is tight, her body so much smaller than my own. The tip slides in without much difficulty but the first ridge presses against her, stopping further progress. I hold, letting her body adjust. She pants, short, fast breaths, biting her lip.

"So big," she says, then nods. "Go on, push, gentle."

Following her lead, I press into her, pushing gently, watching her closely for any sign of anything besides pleasure. She continues panting, her eyes closed, her fingernails digging into my shoulders.

"Errol!" she cries out, as the first ridge passes inside.

It's takes all my will to hold there. She is so warm, her body gripping the first part of my cock tightly, fitting it perfectly as if she was made for me and me alone. She resumes panting, her chest heaving, forcing those beautiful mounds up and down, pressing them into my chest.

"More," she grunts, pushing her hips up against me. "More!"

Her voice and body are demanding. I obey, pressing into her then the second ridge slides in, easier than the first, her body growing accustomed to my girth. My tongue tangles with hers as I push in gently, rocking my hips to make room. Her fingernails dig into me, her breathing increases as I finally seat myself inside her, my hips meeting hers.

We groan as one, and I break the kiss to rest my forehead against hers, trying to catch my breath, to regain my control as she grips my length tightly.

"Errol," Kate murmurs, her hands sliding down to cup my backside, to pull me closer to her. "Move."

I shudder, hanging on to my control by a thin thread. I take a deep breath before I withdraw and thrust back into her, slowly, gently.

My eyes stay on her lovely face, watch the pleasure suffuse it again. The sight of her pleasure immediately increases my own.

This is not simply a physical act. I feel as though our love-making is healing something inside me, restoring a piece of my soul I thought lost. Melding us together, forming a unifying whole rather than two separate beings. Mating. This is a true mating. And I know Kate feels it too.

Her eyes look deeply into my own, her emotions mirroring mine as her fingers caress me. Feather-light strokes over my wings, my scales. A firmer grip on my shoulders, my back. I welcome every touch. Wanting only more. I do not know how I will ever sate myself with her. Perhaps I never will. But I know I will enjoy trying.

I have never felt more complete than in this moment, with her touch sending echoes of ecstasy through my body.

Never felt more connected with anyone. I force myself to stay gentle, to keep up the slow rocking rhythm. Until her hips start thrusting against mine with more urgency. She wants more.

The realization cracks my hard-won control.

With a hoarse sound, I give into the raging fire inside me, my thrusts losing their smoothness as our hips come together in a crashing rhythm that feels like its melding our souls, not just our bodies. I do not doubt that that is what is happening.

When she cries out, her body clenching down on me, I thrust in as deeply as I can, my own pleasure finally over-taking me.

I know I will never be the same.

11

KATE

I admire the way the meteorite glass shimmers in the sunlight, so I crouch next to it. It shimmers as I look at it from different angles, a rainbow of colors overlaid on a darker background. Beautiful. I carefully brush away the sand around the unusually colored glass, picking it out of the hole made by the meteorite. I rub my fingertips over the smoothness of it before adding it to the small collection in my backpack. A few sentimental mementos of my first time with Errol. I never thought I would be so sappy, but here I am. I look up from my bag, my smile fading. I never expected this to happen, not with Errol or anyone else.

I'm definitely on that terrifying, uncertain path I've always been careful to avoid. The one that leads to emotional intimacy...and love. Though that's not right either. I need to be honest with myself. I'm not just on the path that leads to love. I'm already there. I've already fallen head over heels for this honorable, sexy, brave Zmaj. I'm sure it's love, even after knowing him only for a matter of days.

Just as I'm certain in my very bones that Errol is serious about me. And loyal. He's a deeply loyal person I can always trust. As uncertain as I am about everything else, I know Errol's character is beyond reproach. That trust is enough to force me past my internal protections, enough to let myself hope that this thing between us will work out. Will last.

"Kate?" I turn at Errol's voice. "It is time to leave."

I smile at him, I shoulder my backpack, and head over. He smiles back, taking my hand as I reach him. We walk back towards the rover, the sand around us glimmering with pockets of more glass. It really is a sight to behold.

"Is everything fine?" he asks as we slide into the vehicle, his eyes on my face.

"Yes," I reassure him, leaning over to kiss his cheek. "Everything's fine." More than fine. I feel alive in a way I never expected to. He nods, a slight smile curling his lips as he settles back in his seat.

The journey back to the city is vastly different than the one to the rover. For one, it takes a fraction of the time now that we're driving rather than on foot. For another, when Errol and I fall silent, the quiet is comfortable rather than tense.

He holds my hand the whole way back.

When we do arrive at the city, Errol comes with me to go see my friends first. I want to let them know I have the rover back on line. I also let them know that I'm planning to go back to Errol's home with him.

"Oh, cool. Can I come with?" Fallon asks. "I want to see what else is out there."

I look up at Errol. I don't want to invite more people to his little community without a go ahead from him.

"I know anyone who wants to come will be welcome," he reassures her with a smile.

"Can I come too, then?" Nora speaks up in her quiet way. "The city is great, but it's also a little overwhelming."

"Sure," I agree now that Errol has approved. I look around

at the assembled group. "Does anybody else want to check it out too?"

"I think I want to stay here. There's so much amazing Zmaj tech here that needs to be fixed!" Addison explains excitedly. "I really want to work on it, if I can."

It turns out Ashlee wants to stay as well, to help with beautification. When all is said and done, only Fallon and Nora want to tag along. Seems like our little group is already disbanding. The thought is bittersweet, but the small regret isn't anything compared to the brightness of the future we're all looking at now. And I'm so happy to see all of us doing so much better, both in physical health and psychological. I haven't seen everyone so excited in a long time.

"All right. I'm going to meet with Rosalind to update her on everything, and then we'll get ready to go," I tell them. "Be ready."

Errol has already been away from home longer than he expected to be, and there's nothing really holding me here, so we're leaving as soon as we can. The women start to get ready as I leave.

Errol comes with me to seek Rosalind out in her office, but he stays quiet for the most part while we're there.

"I just wanted to thank you for all your help," I say after I hug her. "We wouldn't have made it without you. And Errol," I add, smiling at him.

"It was no problem," Rosalind reassures me. "I'm assuming the rover is up and running?"

I nod, my smile turning into a true grin. "Yes," I say. "Purring like a kitten. Which brings me to the next thing I wanted to tell you—I want to go back with Errol, to the caves. And Fallon and Nora want to come along as well."

Rosalind's incisive gaze shifts from me to Errol and then back again.

"I see." And I think she really does. Then she smiles. "At

least you now have a quicker and safer means of transportation."

I relax a little at her easy acceptance. I didn't know what I expected. Probably I was still too used to Annabel's style of leadership, which had been more bullying than anything.

"True," I agree. "And let me know if you need to use it for something. I'll be more than happy to lend it to you."

"That's a very generous offer. One I'll likely take you up on at some point." Then she cocks her head slightly to the side. "I also wanted to ask...is there anything else you'd like to tell me about how you survived for this long on Tajss?"

Errol spoke to me about Rosalind's desire to know more about our time here and the reasons why. Now that I've experienced having to lead a group myself, and the responsibility it entails, I'm more sympathetic to her desire to keep everyone under her care safe. Heck, I can't imagine having to deal with people on this massive a scale. It would be a whole other ballgame. After seeing how she's dealt with everything so far, I think I can trust her with this.

"We were rescued by a Zmaj after we were attacked by the animals here," I admit. "An elder, one who keeps to himself— a loner I guess. He was generous enough, kind enough to look after us, give us a place to stay and food to eat, though Annabel played the larger regulating role for our group." I pause, considering how my previous reticence may have come off. "I'm sorry for not telling you the whole story before. But I just didn't want to place Gomul in any danger if I could help it. We owe him our lives."

Rosalind sits back in her chair, her face softening as I fill her in.

"I understand," she says gently, seeming disarmed by my open confession. "And I'm glad you feel comfortable enough to tell me now."

I nod, even while I can tell she wants to ask more questions, but she holds herself back. I'm sure she would like a map drawn, to know exactly where this Zmaj is, where the rest of our group are. She's an information junkie, and for good reason, but she doesn't ask for more. I really appreciate that. I wouldn't be comfortable leaving Gomul and the rest of the group so vulnerable. It would feel like I was betraying everyone.

On the other hand, from what I hear, Rosalind wouldn't have a whole lot of time and resources to devote to tracking them down anyway. She apparently already has her hands full dealing with an offshoot of other survivors in a more distant camp, a group that is proving difficult to negotiate with regarding some kind of mining operation. Yeah, I really don't envy her position. We say our goodbyes, and Rosalind wishes us a good trip.

After that, we immediately pack our things, and all the women come with us out to the rover. Those who are staying in the city take the last of their things out of the vehicle. The goodbye is more emotional than I would have expected, all of us hugging each other tight. Venturing out of the tunnels was scary. It's bonded us in a way that I don't think will ever fade, even though we're going our separate ways.

The girls wave at us as we get into the rover and drive away, Fallon and Nora in the back seat. Fortunately, the mood is different from the way we felt when we first left Annabel's tender care. Where the drive out from the tunnels was infused with a lot more fear, this trip feels more like an adventure. Part of it is because we have an actual destination in mind, I'm sure. Mostly it was because I feared the others might all be dead, that my feeling they weren't was just wishful thinking.

I'm sure the others felt the same. But so many people are very much alive! I still can't wrap my head around the people who are here that we didn't know about.

And the communities that have popped up in different areas of Tajss, in a way that gives me real hope for the future, despite the political issues that seem to be looming on the horizon, judging by the events I've been filled in on. Political strife is a part of any society, I guess. We had some on the ship, even. But that right there is the important part, isn't it? We have an actual society in progress here. Somewhere to build a life.

I don't realize I have a smile on my face as I think of that until Errol reaches over to take my hand when I let go of the wheel with one.

"What is it?" he says. "What's made you happy?"

Before I can answer, Fallon and Nora gasp behind us, and I realize this is the first time they've seen an affectionate gesture between the two of us.

"Are you two together? Like *together* together?" Fallon demands, leaning forward.

I feel my face redden at the question even as my smile widens. "Yes," I say simply, turning my hand over to grip Errol's. "We are."

Nora squeals. "Oh, that's so wonderful! Congratulations!"

"Yeah, that's great!" Fallon agrees happily. "Wow, maybe we'll get some hunky Zmaj guys too," she jokes, both of them laughing in the back seat.

I laugh too, shaking my head. I'm so glad they're taking it so well, I can't help but grin. Why had I been scared?

Errol laughs at their antics too, raising my hand to his mouth and kissing the back of it in a gallant gesture that sums up who he is. Our secret is fully out. Not that I intended to keep it under wraps for long. I'm damn proud to be at Errol's side, even if there's a shy, quiet place within me that's only just beginning to inch into our union.

It'll come along. I'm not going to hold back living because of it.

ERROL

I am both excited and nervous to be bringing Kate back to the caves. Excited because she wants to be with me, and nervous because I want her to be happy here, where I have made my home.

'I hope you like it," I say. "We do not have all the amenities of the City, but it is nice. The Tribe, as we call ourselves, used to live further out in the desert in a small canyon."

"Why did you leave?" Kate asks, and the others look interested as well.

"The Zzlo found our home, it was too dangerous to stay there with them knowing where we were," I say. "We had rescued some humans from your ship's wreckage as well. We didn't want to put them at risk."

"You call it the Tribe," Fallon says. "Can you explain that?"

Smiling, I think about how to explain it. It's been so long and so much of the memory of its start is claimed by the bijass.

"After the Devastation there were not many of us left. Those of us who survived found we were suffering from something we call the bijass."

"Bi-jazz?" Nora says, stumbling over the word.

"Bi-jah-sss," I correct her. She says it again, getting it right this time. "We were… retreating? Perhaps this is the best way to say it. Becoming more primal, territorial, there was fighting, often to the death if not stopped by others.

Over time we separated from each other, resigning ourselves to our fate, to wander the desert and die alone. None of our females survived the devastation. There was no future."

"Oh," Kate says, a single syllable that conveys so much more. She places a hand on my arm, squeezing.

"One male, Kalessin, father of Visidion, had a vision. He is gifted in such ways, at times seeing into the future. He gathered those of us he could find and founded the Tribe. He gave us the Edicts. Tools we can use to control ourselves, to push away the bijass."

"Edicts?" Fallon asks, leaning forward, hands on her knees.

"Yes," I nod. "One, I am myself. Two, together we are stronger. Three, survival of the group matters. The Edicts bring us together, bind us, one to another."

"Wow," Fallon says sitting back and shaking her head.

"That's a powerful mantra, if it does all that," Nora observes.

"I think they're beautiful," Kate says, smiling and my hearts race into a gallop.

We continue our ride in an easy silence, each of us consumed by our own thoughts.

When we arrive and exit the rover, I feel like I should not have worried at all. Kate's face is glowing as she looks around.

"Oh, wow! It's gorgeous!" she exclaims, taking my hand.

"Yeah, this is really nice," Fallon says.

"It feels a lot homier than the city," Nora says, nodding.

I feel a cool wash of relief at their positive reactions. It is true. I often feel a bit overwhelmed myself in the city after I spend time here in a smaller group. It feels more personal.

That is all the conversation we have a chance to have as everyone in the Tribe descends upon us.

"Kate!" Delilah cries out, taking her into a hug. "Oh, and Fallon and Nora! Oh my God! I'm so happy to see you guys!"

I smile as the females immediately engulf the newcomers. Their happy chatter eases my heart. I am so glad they are welcoming Kate and the others into the Tribe with genuine enthusiasm.

Melchior slaps me on the back in greeting, while Bashir grabs me in a rough hug.

"Congratulations on your new mate," Bashir says close to my ear, before stepping back, slapping my shoulder, and grinning like a boy. I grin back, not surprised that they drew the correct conclusion from our brief interaction. It is nice to hear, even though it still feels so new, so fragile. Mate. I have a mate. A beautiful, bright, intelligent mate.

I greet everyone, happy to be back. This is home and while being away sometimes is good, I like to be here for the most part. After I have greeted everyone, I retreat to my work station when I see Kate is still in the midst of her reunion, along with meeting others she doesn't know. There is much to do after being gone for days. I should get started, but once I am inside, I cannot seem to concentrate fully, finding myself wandering out to check on Kate after only a short time.

She smiles at me and waves when she sees me, saying something to the other females before breaking away and walking over. Something in me settles as she takes my hand, chattering excitedly as I lead her back to my work room.

"This place is great, Errol! I feel like this is where I really belong. It's so beautiful, and there's nobody ruling with an iron fist, well-meaning or not." She looks over at me apologetically. "Not that I don't like Rosalind, but I'd rather not have someone in that vein, after Annabel, you know? I like that the power is more dispersed here."

I smile. "I understand," I reassure her as I pull her inside. "I do not live in the city either, if you'll notice."

She grins. "True. And I actually have friends here! I think I'll be able to make some new ones too. They're so unpretentious and welcoming."

As I listen to Kate speak, hear her joy and excitement, I'm struck by how taken I am with my new mate. I could listen to her voice all day.

"I'm probably talking too much, aren't I?" she asks, stopping abruptly.

"No," I reassure her with a smile. "I am happy to listen to anything you have to say."

Her smile softens as she closes the distance between us.

"You always say the sweetest things," she coos, smoothing her hands up my chest. "It makes me want to..."

She reaches up, drawing my head down to hers. I hum, meeting her lips with mine. The kiss starts soft, exploring, but the passion builds quickly. Groaning, I slide my hands under her rounded backside and pick her up, walking her over to the workbench. I set her down, lean her back, and open her shirt to close my mouth over one hard nipple.

"Errol!" she cries out, arching up into the touch.

Growling, I reach down to slide my fingers into her pants and underwear, shoving them down impatiently. If I could keep her naked, I would. My fingers slide between her legs, slipping into her damp folds as her hands clutch at my shoulders. She's so soft, so delicate. So wet and ready for me.

I'm panting as hard as she is when I straighten. Her hands

immediately go for my own loin covering, pulling my hard cock out, stroking me firmly. My breath hitches at the intimate touch, at the sight of her pale hands against me. If I didn't feel that driving need, I could luxuriate in that touch for hours. As it is, I push her hands aside and step closer.

"I need to be inside you," I murmur, my hands sliding up the silky smoothness of her thighs. "Now."

"Yes," she sighs, raising her legs and wrapping them around my hips. "Come inside, Errol."

I groan at the invitation, feeling so close to the edge before I even touch my tip to her. She is ready, her wetness coating me as I slowly work myself into her, clenching my jaw to maintain control. I will always have to take care, her smallness something that will not change. I do not mind. Not at all. But her vice grip while I am already so close is torturous. A torture that I would gladly endure again and again.

I try to be gentle after I am seated in the entire way, but Kate urges me to go faster, harder. Until the sound of our bodies' joining is loud, accompanied by her throaty moans and my own low growl. She orgasms quickly, but I grit my teeth and avoid following as she clenches on me. I do not want to come too quickly.

When her eyes open, her hair sticking to the side of her sweaty face, I pick her up and turn her around to bend her over the counter and slide back into her from behind, her backside cushioning my hips. Her waist is small under my hands as I grip her, hold her in place for my thrusts. She is so feminine in every way, so small and delicate, but able to take me, able to take my passion.

I pick her up again, sit down on a chair, and she straddles me, licking her lips as she takes over. I cannot hold back while watching her take her pleasure again, her eyes closing halfway a she holds on tight.

But my second cock is ready to go right after. Kate's eyes

widen at the sight. Fearful that it would be too much for her, knowing through the others that human men do not have two cocks but only one, I had hidden it from her during our earlier lovemaking. But the way she touches it, the way her curious fingers linger, I know I should not have been afraid.

"Two dicks?" she asks, shaking her head with a grin. "Could you be more perfect?" she laughs.

I grin back.

"Not nearly as perfect as you," I say, and then slide back into her, to the sound of her fulfilled sigh. I take her everywhere in my work room, until I know I will never look at the space the same way again. It will always remind me of her, of our time together here. Finally, we end up on a pallet I keep in one section of the room in case I must work into the night.

Kate sighs as she pushes her face into my neck, tucked in close against me. I feel completely empty, my body relaxed and happy. I trail my fingers down her arm, admiring the fine-grained skin.

"Tell me of life on the ship," I murmur, my eyes still on my fingertips as I touch her. When she is near, I want to always be touching her. "What was it like?"

Kate stills, drawing back so she can see my face.

"Hmm. It was...different," she starts, her eyes distant as she remembers. "Definitely more comfortable than Tajss," she says wryly. "But also more boring, you could say." She meets my eyes with a small smile. "I had friends, but I wasn't very social. I was kind of a loner, I guess."

"Hmm." I grip the side of her hip. "Perhaps you were saving yourself for me."

She chuckles, ducking her head back down to press it against my neck.

"Maybe," she sighs, her words a whisper against my neck. "Maybe."

I know I was waiting for her. We stay there, wrapped in

each other's arms, until it is time for the communal meal. I have work to do, but I cannot regret the delay. I would take time with Kate over work any day, but hunger has us rising.

After cleaning up and dressing, I lead Kate over to the food, her small hand familiar in my own. I feel as though I am floating, my joy at having Kate with me softening all my harsh edges.

As we walk into the large room, Melchior deliberately bumps against me, snarling under his breath as he passes by. I immediately feel my bijass rise to the surface at the aggressive sound, at the provoking gesture. I walked away when Melchior approached Kate at Rosalind's party, when I thought Kate did not want me.

It was difficult to step away then when I saw his interest in her. I cannot do so again.

"Melchior," I call out clearly and loudly. "Why do not you join me outside?"

He turns at my voice, his eyes narrowed.

"Of course," he growls in mock politeness. "I would love to."

"Errol, no," Kate urges next to me. I see the alarm in the other females' faces as they try to do the same with Melchior. "Just let it go."

"No," I return firmly, shaking my head. "He needs to be taught to show respect," I growl. And to realize that Kate was never his to begin with.

Despite the females' efforts to defuse the situation, Melchior and I both step outside, the others spilling out with us, still attempting to stop the impending fight.

It is too late.

Melchior snarls and leaps at me as soon as we are outside. Avoiding his fist, I land a hard punch of my own. His head jerks back after the blow connects. Snarling, he rushes at me again.

I start to reach for my knife, but Kate's voice breaks through the haze.

"No, Errol!"

I let go of the hilt and move in with just my fists, Kate's cries helping me keep my head enough not to use lethal force.

He lands a blow, but I'm in a full violent haze and barely feel it as I attack him. It doesn't take long for me to get the clear upper hand, though he refuses to give in. That only tells me I must be harsher in making my point—

Feminine screams have both of us freezing instantly. These are not the ones we've been hearing because of the fight. These are shrieks of terror.

"Guster!" a female screams.

I turn around in horror, just in time to see a guster barreling straight for the group of human females, easily passing through the space in the unfinished wall. The commotion of our fight may have attracted it to us.

Every thought in my mind dies away, and every sight fades but what's in the center of my vision: Kate, directly in the giant lizard's path. Its sharp teeth are exposed, and its predatory eyes are focused on her.

Forgetting Melchior completely, I leap towards her, moving faster than I ever have before in my life.

Kate is my life. She cannot be hurt.

As soon as I reach her, I push her to the side, to safety, just as the guster lunges for me. I leap into the air again, its teeth just barely missing me as it tries to take a bite. Then I am running down its humped back, using the spikes in its thick skin to steady myself when it bucks underneath me.

Cursing, I jump off the thing, rolling to avoid its tail as it whips it at me.

"Errol!"

I look up at Melchior's call, just in time to catch the

lochaber he tosses. I smile grimly. Time to kill this beast. Melchior distracts the guster with his own weapon as I leap onto its back again, bringing the blade up high and slicing down. It isn't the killing blow, but the next one is.

When the guster throws me off, Melchior slashes out one of its eyes. I use the blind spot and its distraction to slit its throat from underneath. It fights for a bit longer, its giant body thrashing as it keeps attacking, but ultimately, it succumbs to its grave wounds and falls to the ground.

I stare at it, my chest heaving from my harsh breath. Shame is a painful and uncomfortable companion as I stare at the beast that almost killed Kate. I must resist the urge to stab it some more, even though it is clearly dead.

How could I have lost control so completely that I left her vulnerable? How could I, myself, have put her in danger? Am I so weak that I cannot even ignore something so small as a sign of disrespect?

Bashir squeezes my shoulder, drawing my attention away.

"Good kill," he murmurs. "We will take care of carving the carcass up for the meat."

I look over at the other Zmaj ready to do just that.

"Thank you," I say. "Together we are stronger."

At least there is a positive to this mess. We now have more food for our growing Tribe. But that is not my concern at the moment.

My eyes scan the group of females, looking for that shock of red hair. There. Kate sits on the ground, the other humans fussing over her.

Clenching my jaw, I stride over, the other females stepping back to allow me room. I do not say anything as I crouch down to pick her up, cradling her carefully in my arms. I must tend to her.

"Errol..." she starts.

I shake my head as I stride quickly to our quarters, where I had already arranged a bath for after dinner. I need to be alone with her to reassure myself that she is fine.

Kate remains silent as I undress her, run my hands over her to ensure she is not hurt.

"I'm fine," she says soothingly. "Really."

I shake my head again, not trusting my voice. Undressing as well, I help her into the bath, taking care to wash her thoroughly, gentle with the scrapes on her lovely skin. Scrapes that I am responsible for. I hate seeing anything marring her. After finishing with the bath, I rub a soothing ointment onto the scrapes and bruises, my fingers gentle, careful.

"I am so sorry losing my head caused you the slightest injury," I finally say hoarsely. "It was not my intention. I should have had better control."

"It's okay," she says, kissing me softly. "I'm not even hurt."

I shake my head. Even the smallest cut is unforgivable when it is there because of me.

"Errol...it's okay," she repeats, turning my head towards her, trailing kisses across my cheeks. "It's okay. I'm fine."

She kisses my forehead. My lips. Pushing at my shoulders, she urges me to lay flat on the pallet, and then proceeds to kiss me everywhere, her soft hands and softer mouth coaxing a response from me easily. I will always respond to her attention. I moan when her hands caress my length. Meet her beloved eyes with my own when her slender body rises above me. She takes me into herself, her teeth sinking into her bottom lip as I spear into her warmth. Then she starts to move, her eyes staying on mine as her body rises and falls above me.

This is not simply lovemaking. It is comfort. Connection. Bonding. Forgiveness. And I can no longer imagine my life without it. Without Kate.

I watch as she rocks herself to her own pleasure, her eyes finally closing with it, her hands coming down to grip my shoulders. The sight of her climax, the feel of her fluttering around me, triggers my own. I shudder with it as she lies down on top of me, setting her lips on mine. I wrap my arms around her, holding her close. Never wanting to let go.

As we relax, other thoughts begin to creep in. Thoughts I did not even realize were plaguing me.

"I think...I believe I am ready to see my father." I do not know I am going to say those words until they are coming out of my mouth. But it is true. The shock of the information has settled sufficiently. I need to go see for myself. Need to meet him. If it is him.

Kate rises, propping herself up on my chest to meet my eyes, her tousled hair framing her pretty face.

"I think that's a good idea," she agrees as I smooth flyaway strands. Her eyes are serious as they look into mine, seeing me as nobody ever has before. Or likely ever will. "I think at least part of your rage must stem from the grief you felt for him, the hurt you swallowed rather than let out at that enormous loss." She slides her hand up to cover my heart. "No one is ever going to take me from you, Errol. Not Melchior or anyone else. I'm yours."

I cup the back of her head, bringing her down to kiss her after that announcement.

"As I am yours," I whisper against her lips.

They curve against mine at my words.

But then she rises slightly.

"You *need* to see your father Errol." She must see some of the anxiety I feel at the thought because she takes my hand in hers, squeezing it in comfort. "I'll come with you." But then she makes a face. "Even if it means facing Annabel sooner than I would really like to."

I chuckle, the last comment lightening the mood some-what. I bury my face in Kate's hair when she lies back down, closing my eyes and breathing in her scent. I know I can do this, and more, with her by my side.

KATE

J pull out another root vegetable, laughing at Delilah's commentary as I work.

"You know what I want to see? Just some plain-ass brown sand. Or, better yet, some actual green grass! Just something not this damn red color!"

"I'd settle for a nice, comfortable seventy-five-degree day," Bailey counters, straightening and wiping at her brow to a chorus of agreement. "I don't remember what it's like not to be hot."

Those are good. I decide to add my own fantasy to the mix.

"You know what I want? A beach. Crystal clear water, palm trees, a cold drink." I sigh, picturing it so vividly, though I've never been to a beach. Heck, before we crashed here, none of had ever been off the ship. But I can imagine the fine-grained sand between my toes, the slight coolness of the water, the ice-cold beverage.... Yeah, I wouldn't say no to any of that.

"That does sound nice," Astrid agrees. "But if we're going to dream big, girls, let's dream big! Add some hotties to the mix." She gives an exaggerated wag of her brows that has us all cracking up again, the conversation devolving from there.

There's a lot of talk of wide shoulders and muscled arms before they start bandying around specifics. I grin as the others sigh over the various movie stars we've seen on the ship's collection of vids, from Ryan Gosling to Henry Cavill to Idris Elba.

But all I can think of is Errol. His handsome face, his pretty scales, his tanned skin, and gorgeous muscles. His sweetness. And courage. The way he looks at me, like I'm the most beautiful woman in the world. I can almost believe it when I see that look in his eyes.

"What about you, Kate?" I look up at Bailey's question. "Who would you have on that beach with you? Young Brad Pitt? Perhaps a Robert Redford?"

"Oooh, what about Gerard Butler from *300*?" Astrid adds. "With the whole getup," she sighs dreamily. "Now there's a *man*!"

I grin at the suggestions, shaking my head. I could just play along, name some random actor and move on. But I don't really want to brush them off like that. I've had so much fun bonding with them, and it's felt so natural...so easy. So different from Annabel's group, where I felt like I was always watching what I was saying. I don't want to mar that feeling by starting off less than honest.

I still feel that flutter of butterflies in my stomach at the thought of revealing what's between Errol and me. It feels like I'm laying my vulnerable, soft underbelly bare and hoping nobody will take advantage of the exposure. It's not a deep, dark secret. Everyone is going to find out soon enough anyway. We have no plans to try to keep it under wraps forever. Here we go. I clear my throat in preparation. Or to delay a little more.

"Actually...I would want just Errol there with me on that beach."

There's a stunned pause at that announcement. Everyone stops what they're doing to turn and look at me, mouths agape. Then the floodgates burst.

"Oh my God! Are you guys actually together?" Astrid asks, everyone else leaning in with expectant gazes.

"Yes, we are," I say, feeling the weight of all that attention. Being the center of everything isn't particularly where I always want to be, but they could not have reacted better.

"Oh man, congratulations!"

"That's amazing!"

"Oh my goodness, that's so exciting!"

I smile at the well-wishes, responding to the rapid-fire questions about where we met, how long we've been together, and so on.

As I'm doing so, I notice that Delilah is maybe smiling a little too hard at the news, the smile looking forced. I don't take it personally though. She's only been nice to me so far. So, I'm guessing the reaction is maybe because she had a crush on Errol, something I certainly couldn't blame her for. From the way she tries to absorb the news and not make a fuss, I know she means well. It doesn't make me regret the uncharacteristic sharing. Not with the burgeoning sisterhood feel between all of us already.

When they close around me in their excitement, I feel like the confession has only drawn us closer. I truly treasure that closeness. I want more female friendships. Ever since the ship crashed here, I've been unhappy because I missed out on that part of life. Maybe now is the time to make up for that.

The distraction of all the women also helps me with the worry that coils in my gut at the prospect of facing off with Annabel again. I'm glad I was able to come here before having to go back to the tunnels. I needed this respite, a chance to recharge, and now I know what it's like here with the Tribe as well.

Some of the ones who stayed might come back with me when they realize there's a city and this community, both of them quite nice. It's just the kind of thing that could possibly shake them out of the rut of going along with whatever Annabel wants, like they've been doing so far. The fact that there's something more out here will instill confidence in something else, perhaps open the door to trust someone other than their current "guide."

Because, the truth is, Annabel's been unraveling since the death of her husband, slowly but surely. With the distance I have now, that reality has never been so glaringly clear. I don't even want to think about what it must be like to live with her these days, after the added anger and bitterness of us leaving. The idea that I could challenge her authority— that all of us could leave in front of everyone was a huge blow to her ego.

We didn't come running back right away, so she's likely to be feeling insecure now, even if most of the group stayed behind with her. Maybe she just told everyone that we met a gruesome end (that we deserved, of course) and that's why we didn't come crawling back. So if I show up again now, alive and well, that will really mess with the story she's been telling.

But I happily put thoughts of Annabel aside for the moment as the women continue to ply me with questions while we work. The day passes quickly even though we're working the entire time. Just goes to show how much good company really does matter.

Then it's time for the communal dinner. We have plenty of meat to feast on, now that Errol and the other Zmaj managed to quash their differences and kill the attacking beast. At least something good came out of that fight, though

I don't really blame Errol. He's obviously been through a lot and he's been trying his best. I don't like that he makes himself feel so guilty over it. He's being too hard on himself.

Like I've conjured him through my thoughts, Errol finds me and sits next to me at dinner, smiling at me and taking my hand in his. I smile back happily, more content in that moment than I ever thought I could be. Not just here on Tajss, but ever. The food is delicious, the company is wonderful, and I have Errol by my side. I try to take it all in, to live in that moment.

Afterwards, Errol stands. "Would you like to go for a walk?" he asks, a slight smile on his face.

"Sure," I say, taking his hand and letting him draw me to my feet. "A walk sounds nice."

So we meander over to the still unfinished wall, where Errol stops.

"One moment please," he says.

"Sure," I say, wondering what this is about.

Then he leaps into the air, using his wings to jump higher than I thought was possible. His head swivels at the apex of his leap, his eyes sharp as he scans. After a moment, he drops back down gently, bending his knees as his feet hit the sand.

"Sorry, I wanted to be sure there is no danger nearby," he explains, taking my hand again. "I will not take a chance again."

It's a sobering thought, but he's right. I've seen too much here to take safety for granted, even now when I'm feeling the most relaxed. After we start walking again, I can tell that his mood has turned and he's thinking of something not altogether pleasant, something that troubles him.

"What is it, Errol?" I ask, tightening my hand on his. "What are you thinking about?"

He sighs, squeezing my hand back.

"It still shakes me to the bone to think I might have lost

you because I was so stupidly distracted," he confesses, turning to meet my eyes. "It was so close to happening..."

The anguish on his face tears me apart inside. I shake my head, lifting my hand to stroke the side of his face.

"You don't have to keep beating yourself up over that," I say. "I'm okay. Because of you, I might add."

There's no doubt of that. If he hadn't been so quick, hadn't shoved me out of the way just in time...

His eyes darken, speaking to the deepest parts of me. The parts that are just as full of fear, looking back at that moment.

"I do not know what I would have done if..."

He doesn't finish the sentence as he lifts me into his arms, my legs wrapping automatically around his waist.

"Kate..." he whispers, a volatile mix of emotions in his eyes.

One I can fully relate to. The kiss that follows is deep, almost desperate, and takes all my attention. I don't even notice he's walking us back to our quarters, don't even think to check if anyone is watching. I only realize we've changed location when he's laying me back down on the bed, his eyes glittering in the dark.

The lovemaking that follows is slow but hard, his hands hot and greedy in the best way. He touches me everywhere. Kisses me everywhere. By the time he's pushing himself into me, his hands pushing my legs wide, I'm well past the point of ready. The climax that follows is deep, all-encompassing. Necessary. Errol shudders on top of me, his own eyes closing with his pleasure on the heels of mine. But when his eyes open, he doesn't withdraw or lower himself on top of me.

"Kate...I know you are mine," he says, his voice husky and deep. "I know...you are my mate."

His eyes are vulnerable as he watches me, as though he thinks I might hurt him now that he's laid his heart bare to me. I melt at his words. At the depth of feeling clear in his eyes.

I know I will forever remember this warm, quiet night.

"Errol..." I sigh, pulling him down to kiss him softly, saying everything I have to say with that meeting of mouths —the depth of my feelings, the passion I feel for him, the fear. I have so much more to lose now.

He groans, kissing me back even more forcefully, meeting my passion with his own. I feel him nudging me with his other cock. Still rock hard.

"Kate," he murmurs, pushing into me once more.

"Yes," I sigh, holding him close.

The round that follows his confession leaves me deliciously sore and thoroughly sated.

ERROL

When Rosalind finds out Kate and I are planning on going to visit the Zmaj that helped Kate and her group survive, Rosalind sends word that she wants to meet with me first. I understand her perspective and agree. This will be the first time one of our own group is going to make contact, so it's only prudent we keep her apprised as well.

"I'm coming with you," Kate insists when I tell her I must make a trip to the city before we can leave on our own.

"You are welcome to come." I would be happy to have her always with me. "But it is not necessary if you would like to remain here." I can see how well she is adjusting, how much she likes the other females here. It warms my heart. I want her to be comfortable and content. I do not want to force her where she does not want to go.

"No, it makes sense for me to go," she counters. "That way we can just leave for the tunnels right after. There's no point in delaying the trip. It'll only give both of us more time to worry."

That is sound reasoning. I do not want to fight her joining me. So we leave the Tribe after some quick goodbyes and climb into the rover to head to the city.

"I have to admit," I say as I settle into the seat, "this vehicle is spoiling me for foot travel."

Kate grins and says, "You and me both," as she presses on the accelerator.

The ride to the city is pleasant and uneventful, the rover eating up the distance without a problem. I'd never know it had been broken. I feel a burst of pride. My mate is a female of great skill, skill that I cannot help but admire.

"Here we are," she says when we arrive at the city a short time later. "I wonder what Rosalind wants to speak to us about."

I can hear a slight touch of nerves in her voice, but not too much. Kate is a strong person in her own right. I know she would not be overwhelmed by Rosalind and her commanding presence.

As soon as we enter the city, we go directly to Rosalind's office, where she is waiting for us.

"Thank you for coming," she says with a smile, gesturing for us to sit. "How are you doing? How is the Tribe treating you, Kate?"

"Good," Kate murmurs, smiling back. "Really good."

I can see that her guard is up. With a jolt, I realize I no longer see that wall around me. Isn't that wonderful?

"That's great," Rosalind remarks, settling her entwined hands on her desk and leaning slightly forward. "I'm glad to see you so happy with your new living arrangements. Now, on to business and why you're here." She looks over at me and then back at Kate. "I just wanted to touch base with you before you head back to your group, Kate. I have some requests."

"What kind of requests?" I ask. I knew there must be some, or she wouldn't have asked us to meet with her. Kate's lack of surprise is also clear.

"I want you to send Annabel and her group orders from me. They must join our group here in the city. Once here, they can of course decide to go to your community if they would prefer, just as you have," she says, nodding at Kate. "I would also like to ask permission to use the rover for trips back and forth to the mine and the village there, to check on the other survivors."

There is a small pause as Kate watches the other woman. I can see her processing the information and deciding what to do with it, taking her time with her response despite the pressure I know she feels. I have a feeling Rosalind is lucky to have couched both of her requirements as requests.

"I would be happy to lend the rover for you to use on those trips," she finally says carefully.

"Thank you."

"But I do not feel comfortable commanding the other women to come back. Annabel will not take kindly to that." The wry tone in Kate's voice signals how much of an understatement that was.

"The order would come from me," Rosalind counters. "And if the other women come, even Annabel will surely follow."

Kate shakes her head. "You don't understand the climate over there. I'll pass a message along to Annabel, even though I'd prefer as little contact with her as possible. But I won't order anybody to do anything. They'll come back if they want to. I refuse to involve them in politics I don't even entirely understand myself yet." Her voice is strong, sure. She is standing by her convictions, another thing I admire about her.

I do not know if Rosalind will feel the same way. I watch her behind her desk, wondering what she will have to say to this clear refusal. Hmm. I can see she is not angry. In fact, there is a blooming of real respect in her eyes for Kate's refusal. As one leader to another, I know she can sympathize with my mate's desire to do what's best for her people, even if it is difficult for her.

"I see," Rosalind says, nodding sagely. "Well then. I thank you for your help." She stands up, taking both of us in. "And I would also like to wish you a safe journey tomorrow."

"Thank you," I say, along with Kate, who speaks a brief beat behind me, as if somewhat surprised at Rosalind's calm response.

We do not linger after the dismissal. Rosalind is busy. I know she must have a great deal scheduled after us. Kate waits until we are outside again to voice her inner thoughts.

"I didn't expect Rosalind to react like that to my refusal," she says in a low voice. "It threw me off in a big way."

"How did you expect her to react?" I ask, curious. I have not seen Rosalind be unreasonable. Not in front of Kate or otherwise.

She shrugs. "I don't know. I thought...I thought she was trying to make me into her subject, willing or not." She looks up at me, a self-deprecating smile on her face. "I wonder if I'm just looking for the worst in her because of the triggers Annabel created in me."

"Perhaps," I agree. "Though Rosalind is an often tough leader, I have not found her to be unfair. Or someone who forces her will on others unless absolutely necessary."

Kate nods thoughtfully.

"Maybe she isn't so bad," she agrees slowly. "She's definitely managed to accomplish a lot here on Tajss."

Her words may sound grudging, but I can see she means

them. Nobody can spend an extended amount of time with Rosalind and not admire her. I feel the same about Kate. I'm glad to see this mutual respect developing between them. It bodes well for the future of their relationship.

That night, we visit the other females in Kate's group, as we will be leaving in the morning.

"Oh, and they gave me full access to help work on the ancient tech!" Addison exclaims, giddy with joy over the news. "Isn't that great? And..."

As she continues to chatter on excitedly, I take a step back, feeling as though I've been dealt a blow, a completely unexpected one. The tech...

I have a flash of memory, quickly suppressed. I do not want to think about the past, when tech was freely available. This conversation is triggering too many memories I would rather leave buried, never to emerge.

"I am going for a walk," I say to Kate, attempting to keep my anxiety off my face and not knowing if I have succeeded.

She looks over at me with a frown, but I do not stop to explain. I need to leave, need to escape from this talk that triggers memories best left alone. I leave the room and hurry down the hall. My strides eat up the distance, no clear destination in mind as I run from my own thoughts, until I find myself at the edge of the city, nobody outside at this time of night to witness my irrational episode.

Will there ever be a time where I can listen to these kinds of conversations without fear? Or will I forever be running from my own memories? Attempting to bury a past that keeps reemerging? I do not know. I lower myself onto a bench, lost in myself.

That is how Kate finds me later, sitting alone at the edge of the city. Still trying to make sense of everything. She sits down next to me, her hand sliding down my arm in comfort.

"Hey," she greets me softly. "What's wrong? Why are you upset?"

I shake my head, but she reaches over and turns my head towards hers so that I must meet her eyes. So that I cannot avoid her.

"You can tell me," she murmurs, that sincerity in her eyes almost painful. "Maybe I can help. Let me at least try." That she cares for me, deeply and genuinely, is clear. I am certain that with her voice, with that look in her eyes, she could make almost anyone lay their troubles at her feet. That is a seduction all its own, the gentle suggestion to reveal all that I cannot deny.

I am no exception. I have no protection, no armor against the heartfelt plea. I slide my fingers through her silky hair to cup the back of her head.

"I find myself...almost fearful of seeing my father," I say. It is the first time I have admitted this aloud to another soul.

"What?" Kate says. "I thought you were happy to find out that he is alive. Why would you be fearful?"

If only it were so simple. I sigh, looking away from her eyes again, out into the vastness of the desert. I cannot see her watching me while I speak of this.

"My father and I—My father did not agree with the choices I made before the Devastation." That is the gentlest way I know of describing his utter shock and disgust at what I had decided to do.

Kate is silent for a little while.

"I can't believe that your choices could have been so terrible," she says. "You're such a good person, Errol. I'm reminded of that time and time again. What did you do that he not agree with? Was there some kind of misunderstanding?"

Misunderstanding? Perhaps. Not in my father's eyes.

I swallow, trying to beat back the memories. They are

growing ever more stubborn in their desire to rise up, in their fight to insinuate themselves into life again. Although it feels as though their full reemergence may be inevitable, I refuse to allow them to simply engulf me, take me over, and destroy me, as they threatened to do in my past.

"I do not know how much you have learned of our history so far," I start, after wrestling those dark pieces of the past. "But the Devastation, the conflict that led us from our peak to the desolation now...it started with epis."

"Epis?" Kate asks. "How? How could something so wonderful cause all this."

"It is wonderful," I agree. "Perhaps too wonderful."

"What do you mean?" she whispers.

"Tajss is the only planet where epis grows. But that does not mean others did not also desire to reap the benefits it provides." I shift restlessly. "Tajss became the sole supplier of epis for many different worlds," I explain. "But...we soon became consumed by their need, enslaved by it. So we voted. And decided to rebel, to cease supplying it."

"But epis is addictive," Kate says in low voice. "Oh...no." She understands where this story must end.

"Yes," I say. "When we revolted, refused to supply it any longer, there were many unhappy off-worlders."

"Oh, Errol," Kate says, her eyes wide.

"It was clear we were nearing a disaster, one of catastrophic proportions. If the off-worlders did not get their doses, they knew they were facing certain death."

"Which meant they had nothing to lose," she says quietly.

"Exactly." I frown as I think back on that time. "War was looming. A great one. I did not know how we were going to resolve it. But I did know we needed more time. More time in which I hoped a solution would be found." I take a deep breath and let it out. "So...I formed a group to harvest epis.

To supply the plant to those off-worlders who were threatening us."

"So that you could delay the attacks."

"Yes," I agree. "In the hopes they would at least be temporarily mollified, though it was a losing battle. But my father—" I get a sharp flash of the look on his face when he realized it was me supplying our then-enemies with the life-giving plant, and the image affects me like a blow to the gut. "He thought it was a betrayal of our people. That I had turned my back on my own."

"Oh, Errol." I can hear the heartbreak in her voice for me. "Didn't you tell him what you were trying to do?"

I think back to the confrontation, to his refusal to listen. He would not entertain any reason that could explain my actions in a less negative light.

"He did not want to hear what he thought of as excuses," I explain, thinking back to that moment, when I felt as though the world was falling out from beneath my feet. "He would not even let me try."

And then, the world ended. My small group alone could not keep everyone supplied with epis indefinitely. Not when there were entire planets who had become dependent. We may have delayed the war, but we could not stop it. Looking back, I do not think anyone or anything could have.

"Errol," Kate sighs, her hand sliding down to my chest. "That's terrible."

"I regret not trying harder to fix things between us, to heal the rift before—before it was too late. Before everything was gone."

"That is not your fault. You couldn't control when things deteriorated, couldn't have known it would come to this." Her fingertips grip me tighter. "It isn't too late now. You have a second chance. One that you can make the most of."

A second chance. I roll that phrase around in my mind.

Yes, it appears I do have a second chance. Will it help? I do not think Kate understands the enormity of what happened, how enraged Father was. How hurt. The father I could always count on for sage advice, the friend who would calmly listen as I aired my thoughts, had disappeared in that instant he realized what I'd done. When I do not reply, she continues more briskly.

"Okay. There's nothing to forgive here, though you need to take the chance to try to explain your intentions. You're not going to feel better until you meet with Gomul, because you won't know if you can fix this until you try." She steps in front of me and crouches down, taking my hands in her small, soft ones. I sometimes wonder how someone so soft and small can have such a solid core of strength in her. "I also want to tell him of our mating," she adds with a small, hopeful smile. "And if there are any fences to mend, we will mend them together. I promise."

I feel my heart fill at her words. I have never had someone care about me so deeply before or support me in such an unwavering manner. But, again, she does not understand how badly I disappointed my father.

"Kate..." I start.

"No, Errol," she interrupts, gently but forcefully. "We're going. Heck, I'm even willing to face my down my own nemesis to do it. That's how much I care. How much I know you need this."

It is clear her resolve will not be shaken. I cannot be more forceful in my refusal, not to her, not to my mate, whom I only want to speak soft words to. I would give her anything that is in my ability to gift her. Even this.

"As you wish," I agree simply.

Her face softens at my acquiescence. Wrapping her arms around my shoulders, she leans her face against mine, feathering a kiss over my ear.

"Everything will be okay," she murmurs. "You'll see."

I want to believe her. I wrap my arms around her slender waist, her closeness comforting me in a way nothing else can.

And I hope.

Hope fervently that she is right.

KATE

*T*he suns beat down on the rover, turning the inside of the vehicle into an oven—one set on broil. I wipe at the sweat stinging my eyes, but don't bother with the rest. I'll only be wet with sweat within five minutes again.

"Why are the internal temperature controls not working?" Errol asks. "Did we not pack in enough refuse for fuel? I know it is not a lack of sunlight for the panels," he adds raising a brow as he glances out at the sun-drenched landscape.

I can tell the question isn't because he is uncomfortable, though I don't doubt he is. No, he's been watching me wipe at my face for the last half hour, the blistering heat making me a sopping mess in no time flat.

"The fuel panels are using all the energy converted from the light and the trash to run the engine right now," I explain. "There's nothing left for the AC." And doesn't that just suck. I wipe at my eyes yet again, then pick up the water container and take a few big gulps. What I don't need right now is to become dehydrated, though I feel a whole lot better than I would have without that dose of epis. That plant really is a life saver.

"To the left," Errol says after a few more minutes. "There is a small spring not far off."

I nod, immediately adjusting our course. We've been stopping every so often at the water sources en-route to cool off. It's a necessity in this heat, at least for me. Stopping near the newest set of sparse trees, I stay in the rover as Errol leaves to do a quick recon of the area first. He insists on doing so at every oasis we've stopped at. I know it matters, even if all I want to do is jump directly into the water. I don't want to risk either of us simply because I'm impatient. So I wait until he reappears and nods at me before I exit the rover and head over to the crystal-clear spring. I will say this for Tajss: because all the water is filtered through sand and rock, it's always clean and sparkling. Not that murky water would have stopped me in this heat, but it is nice.

Not bothering with fully stripping like I did in the first couple of stops, I just take off my shoes and walk right into the water. There's no point in taking my clothes off—they'll either be wet with water or wet with sweat. At least they'll be cleaner this way. And it isn't like I'm going to catch a chill.

I sigh as the coolness of the water slowly cocoons me. If I could, I'd just stay here all day. But the real world awaits and so on. Damn it.

I take a deep breath and hold it, close my eyes, and fully submerge myself, using my fingers to scrub at my hair to get the sweat out. I smooth my hair back as I come up, scrubbing at myself with my hands under the water. It's the best I'm going to do for now. We still have a ways to go, and I don't want to waste too much time on these stops. As soon as I've accomplished the bare minimum and cooled off, I step out of the water, wringing out my hair to let it air dry. I wonder if—

A high-pitched shrieking sound has my head jerking up to scan the sky above. What the hell was that? I take a step back as I spot a backlit shape.

It's a huge birdlike creature, circling right above me. That can't be good. I have no idea what it is, but its predatory, sharp-featured face and huge claws don't make me think it's exactly friendly.

"Errol," I say in a low voice, my eyes staying on the threat. "What is that?"

With another shriek from its dark, curved beak, it dives, tucking its enormous wings against its sides and plummeting through the air, its razor-like claws extended and aimed right at me.

"Shit!"

I turn and run, though there isn't much cover to be found. I hear another shriek, this one even closer. There's no way I can outrun something on wings!

"Ooof!"

My breath rushes out of me in a harsh rush as a steel bar hits me in the stomach and then wraps around my waist. Errol's arm. I gasp, reaching down to grip his forearm as he leaps towards his weapon, set down some feet away in preparation for his own swim.

"Hold on!" he shouts, grabbing the weapon and leaping straight up into the air with me still in tow. Oh man. I feel my rations trying to come back up as the altitude changes fast, the constriction of Errol's arm still squeezing around my waist. I swallow hard and visualize keeping the food down. Not coming up. Nope. No no no. It works. Barely. Meanwhile, Errol isn't playing.

He flares out his own wings and swings his lochaber in a deadly arc, the bladed end hitting the bird dead on. It screams as the blade slices into its side, turning hard and dislodging the weapon to dive back at us, its sharp beak open wide, feet extended towards us.

Errol isn't fazed.

Flapping his wings to stay aloft, he stabs straight at the bird's underbelly before its claws can reach us, slicing down the length of it in a hard cut that guts the thing in midair. The bird stops, held a couple of yards away by the lochaber's own length. Errol yanks the blade out with a gush of blood. I wince at the sound. And then the bird's wings slowly crumple until it falls out of the sky right in front of us.

Errol brings us down much more gently, his arm relaxing around me as we touch down on the ground. I take in a much-needed deep breath, my heart still pounding.

"Are you well?" he asks, turning me around to give me an all-encompassing glance.

I nod, still trying to process everything. The attack was lightning fast, the actual fight short and decisive. It all happened in a blink.

"Come, let us continue on," he says, taking my hand as he scans the sky above. "It was my mistake not to look up as well as around, even though vtaks should not be out with the suns still shining so brightly."

I let him lead me back to the rover. Putting some metal between us and any threats sounds perfect right about now.

"Shouldn't we recover the meat?" I ask, looking over at the carcass. I've had it instilled in me here on Tajss to never waste a kill. It's wasteful when food isn't easy to come by. But Errol just shakes his head at my question rather than stopping.

"No. The meat of the vtak tastes too gamey," he explains calmly. Like he engages in these sorts of heroics every day. Right. Totally casual. All right then.

I glance back at the bird, the fact that I almost died— again—finally sinking in. What would I have done without

Errol here? The answer to that is painfully clear. I look away from the bird, taking in Errol's clean profile. He's already saved me so many times. Grateful doesn't even begin to cover how I feel.

Even if he acts like it is a commonplace occurrence.

ERROL

"We're almost there," Kate says next to me, the trepidation plain in her voice. A deep vertical line shows between her brows as she looks out. I sympathize with her worry, though my reason is different. My stomach clenches tight with anxiety as I realize the reprieve of the actual journey is over. Now I must face my past, face one of the memories that has plagued me so in the flesh. I do not know how so much joy and anticipation can coincide with such deep apprehension. But they both swirl inside me at the thought of seeing my father.

How will he receive me after so much time? What if he does not want to see me at all? Is not willing to listen to me still, even after everything that has occurred? What if he rejects me completely?

Kate may have an optimistic view of this meeting, but he could very well refuse to engage with me. That possibility haunts me the closer we get to our destination. If he does refuse to speak with me, I cannot force him to. I cannot force him to accept me. Oh, how much I want my father back in my life! I want that steady, loving presence that I remember before my choices tore us apart.

"Uh...Errol?"

I am so worried about the approaching reunion that I do not notice the danger until Kate's words alert me, bring me back to reality, back to the present.

On the other side of the rover's windshield, a massive head with a short muzzle lowers in front of us, framed by a thick white mane. Slit-pupil eyes peer through the glass. The suns shine against the tough, leathery gray skin, picking out its craggy texture. A mouth opens to reveal razor-sharp teeth, and a deep red tongue flicks out to taste the air.

It is a chatteron. An odd clicking sound from its throat immediately raises my hackles. They make that sound when alerting others of danger. Or prey.

"What do I..."

Kate's question trails off as another creature appears from behind a large rock formation, clearly responding to the clicking alert. Its eyes immediately lock on us as well. I do not need to tell Kate that this is not good.

The second one starts to move towards us, it's loping gait almost lazy as its bird-like paws hit with ground-trembling force. The one in front of us lets out a low rumble, perhaps to encourage the other. It's not in any kind of hurry. They are too close.

Even if Kate pushes the rover, they will catch us at this distance. They are too large for the rover to run over one, let alone two of them. I calculate all this quickly, my mind running through the facts and arriving at the inevitable conclusion.

Kate. Kate must get away.

I reach back and grab my lochaber as I bark out orders.

"Reverse! Accelerate as hard as you can!" I open the door.

"Wait! Where are you going?" she demands frantically,

reaching over clasp her hand over my forearm in a surprisingly strong grip.

"I will distract them while you escape," I say grimly, squeezing her hand briefly before peeling it off firmly. "There is no time to argue. Go!"

I step out of the rover and shut the door over Kate's protest. There is no more time to spend on talking if she is to survive—and she will survive. I will see to it.

I swing the lochaber in a circle, adjusting my grip so I can hold it in both hands. This is not a fight I can win. But sometimes winning is not the prize, is it?

Taking a bracing breath, I launch myself toward the chatterons, using my wings to help me leap faster. I push my body hard, the base of my wings burning, my thighs coiling hard as I land only to jump once more. The faster I close the distance, the farther away they will be from the rover and Kate when I head them off, giving Kate the best chance of escape. The thought of her adds that extra bit of speed that I can never achieve otherwise.

I reach the first one. It does not bother to slow its stride at my appearance. In fact, it is going significantly faster.

I grip the lochaber tightly, angling my body to slide down low, barely avoiding its snapping teeth. I slice at one of its legs with my blade as I push through the front ones. It roars at the cut but swings around easily as I come out behind it, traversing the entire length of its body.

The cut was not deep enough to impede its movement, but I have successfully diverted its attention from the rover, which was my main goal, so I count it a success.

Run, Kate!

It snaps at me again, but I am not there, I am running towards the second one. It slows, glancing between me and the rover, as if it is now uncertain which to choose. I need to help it make up its mind.

It turns its head back towards the rover. No. I increase my speed, the other chatteron on my heels. That one has no trouble deciding which of us to target. Now that I have wounded it, it will not cease until it has me between its jaws. I can feel its hot, moist breath as it nears, gaining ground with its much longer stride.

I leap, flaring out my wings to help give me lift. I land on the second one's back and run up its spine to its head. With a grunt of effort, I swing the lochaber up and slam the butt of it down on the back of its thick skull.

A resounding crack and the reverberation that travels through the staff of the weapon and into my arms signals a direct, forceful hit. The beast shudders under me, feeling the impact keenly as it comes to a halt. It rears back its head and I lose my balance, falling onto my back and cracking my head. Stars dance across my vision as I scrabble to stay on top, but I find no purchase.

Sliding off the side, I slam to the ground, knocking the wind out of myself. The ground trembles and I know the other one is rushing after me. I hear the huff of its breath and climb unsteadily to my feet, knowing I will likely be too late, but satisfied that Kate will escape with her life.

That is my only goal at this point.

I watch as it opens its mouth wide, displaying its glistening teeth. Its neck is already pulled back in preparation for the strike.

I bring my lochaber up horizontally, my only defense, and a meager one at that. My hearts are pounding, my grip slipping slightly from my own sweat. But I refuse to simply give up. The chatteron will have to work for its meal today, because I will not be soft food.

I brace myself, knowing this is likely the end, but determined to inflict damage, to keep the attention on me as long as possible. I am ready, fully committed to what is about to happen as the stink of its rotting previous meal wafts over me.

Just as it lurches to the side.

I blink at the unexpected reprieve, my body moving before I know what's happened. I leap off the back of the chatteron, flaring my wings to slow my descent.

I land in a crouch, my eyes meeting Kate's determined ones through the rover's windshield.

The back of the rover is still up against the chatteron's leg, a slight dent in the body where she hit it. And probably saved my life.

What is that that vehicle made of?

I shake my head at her, panic bursting in my chest. She should already be a safe distance away!

"Move!" I yell at her, waving my arms. "Go!"

The beast could step on her, swipe the vehicle and send it rolling, rendering it useless. Kate wastes no time following my order, the vehicle scooting away quickly as the irritated beast turns to her. It is favoring the leg she hit. Perhaps it is not simply irritated but wounded. Good.

Unfortunately, the distraction takes my attention away from the danger of the second chatteron. A heavy weight crashes into my side, throwing me a good distance away.

Have I learned nothing about a battle? The first rule we learn as children is to never let down our guard, never allow ourselves to be distracted from our opponents. But that rule didn't take Kate into account.

I struggle to breathe as I land hard on the sand, calling myself all sorts of names as I turn just in time to avoid damage to my wings. The landing still hurts, though. I feel as though I need help to fully re-inflate my smashed lungs. But I do not have time to catch my breath, not with a chatteron coming straight at me. I struggle to my feet. I am slow. I am feeling the blow I took. I can barely breathe. Waiting until the last second, more out of necessity than real planning, I dive out of the way, the large creature sweeping just past me. It passes so close that the wind it makes ruffles my hair.

I use the moment it needs to regroup to rush past it, straight to the one still chasing Kate. It does not take long for the one who just missed to turn and follow me again, its lumbering footsteps loud and much too familiar at this point.

I watch, horrified, as the other chatteron nears the rover, its long stride eating up the distance even though Kate is obviously pushing her vehicle as hard as she can.

I am not going to make it in time. That is clear. Still, I refuse to give up.

Legs and lungs burning, I try to squeeze every last ounce of speed out of my body, but it is as though I am not moving at all.

I calculate the distance between the chatteron and the rover. It diminishes rapidly even as I watch. Two more strides. Two more strides and it will be able to topple the thing with a push from its head or a kick from its meaty leg. With Kate inside.

I blink as something suddenly shades my eyes from the glaring light of the suns. Then I see a shadow gliding above me, wings spread. What...?

I look up but cannot see well when the sunlight is no longer obstructed by the form. I shift my attention when the dark shape lands on the back of the chatteron chasing Kate. It is a fellow Zmaj warrior. Hope flares inside me.

He rises from his crouch and stabs down at the thick skull with the blade of his weapon, the sun finally shining directly on his face.

A painfully familiar face.

I stumble, but quickly right myself again. My eyes widen as I watch my father run down the creature's back, his weapon coated in blood, his body as agile as I remember.

It's as if no time at all has passed. The decades apart dissolve as I watch him, my mind almost separating from my body as it continues to move of its own accord.

Then my eye falls on the rover again, and I am firmly back in my body. I cannot be anywhere else until Kate has made it to safety, despite her apparent efforts to avoid just that outcome.

Father has wounded the creature, badly, but it is not done fighting yet, and the one following me is still in perfect health.

Leaving the other to Father, I whirl around and run right back at the other beast, freed from having to worry about them both at once. The beast does not expect the abrupt change in direction. It is unable to stop its forward momentum as I run under its head and stab upwards, as hard and deep as I can from that angle.

The blade jerks forward with my own forward momentum, cutting a deep slice, blood spilling out onto the sand in a hot rush. I jerk my weapon out, tasting iron as I scramble to get out from under the beast while its great body shudders above me. Now that I can focus on one alone, I have an actual chance to succeed. With that in mind, I focus, cutting out all other distractions.

Moving quickly, I slice at the back of the chatteron's legs to hinder movement, stab at its vulnerable underbelly as it slows from blood loss. Eventually, all the wounds add up, big and small, until even a beast that large cannot continue on.

The chatteron slowly falls to the ground, its eyes still focused on me even as the light inside them fades. I do not wait to see more. As soon as that threat is gone, I search for the rover.

There. It's positioned some distance away, seemingly whole and relatively undamaged.

The remaining chatteron falls even as I turn to search for

it next. Father stands silhouetted on top, riding the creature down to the ground, his lochaber buried deep. He pulls it out with a hard jerk once it lands.

The rover's door opens and Kate steps out, her eyes scanning me before going to Father. I walk over to her, still feeling the rage of the battle pumping through my veins.

"Are you hurt?" I ask when I reach her, my eyes searching her body for any sign of new wounds.

"No," she says, hugging me back when I wrap my arms around her. "Not a scratch, thanks to you and Gomul. What about you?" she asks, pulling back. "Are you hurt?"

"Nothing more than bruises," I reassure her. Which is a miracle in and of itself. If my father had not arrived when he did-- I turn as I hear his footsteps nearing, almost as if I've summoned him. His face is reserved, his eyes focused on me. Is he happy to see me? Simply surprised? Or something more negative? There is no way to tell what he is thinking.

"Thank you, Gomul," Kate offers as he nears. "I don't know what we would have done without you. How did you know we needed help?"

"I was keeping watch on the chatterons, making certain they did not become a danger to us in the tunnels," he explains, turning his attention briefly to her. "I am glad that I was."

That statement could be directed at Kate alone. This is not the reunion I would have hoped for, even apart from the fight for our lives, which I suppose would be reason enough. Perhaps I need to put myself forward first. Letting go of my hold on Kate, I take a step towards him.

"Thank you, Father," I say, when he meets my eyes again. "I...it is good to see you."

I take another step forward, wondering if he will reject me, if I came all this way simply to find I should not have bothered after all. That fear is a pit in my stomach.

But, to my amazement he does not rebuff me. Taking a step to meet me in the middle, he silently pulls me into a tight hug, holding me close.

"Likewise, Son."

I shut my eyes tight at the acknowledgment, overcome. He lets me go after a long moment, turning away.

"Come. I do not want to remain here in the open if there are more in their group I have not yet seen. Let us take shelter inside."

"Why don't we just take the rover in?" Kate says. "I need to get it to shelter too."

He looks over at the vehicle. "Very well," he agrees easily.

We all get into the rover, the strangeness of having my father so close not dissipating as we drive the short distance remaining. Is this how we will be around each other now? Slightly formal, somewhat tense? Is this all that is left for us?

"Here we are," Kate says next to me.

The nerves again replace the relief of survival in her voice as she guides the rover into a shaded entryway that leads down. She stops it not far down the steep path.

"Don't want to freak anyone out by going in too far," she says, giving me a strained smile before opening the door and stepping out.

Fair enough. I open my own door and step out with her, my eyes adjusting to the relative dimness.

Just then, a group of females arrive, brandishing an array of weapons.

"Stay back!" the one in front warns, her eyes focused on me. "We will use lethal force!"

Ah. This must be Annabel. Her hair is a bright, sunlight color, her face showing the same pale thinness that Kate's did when I first met her. She is clearly stiff with fright, but she has donned a brave face and is nevertheless at the front of the group, a quality I can appreciate—despite what other characteristics she lacks.

One would be intelligence, clearly. I arrived with Kate and Gomul, both of whom she must know. Is this only posturing?

When I glance at the other human females, they appear equally weak and unhealthy. It truly is a testament to them they have managed to survive so long without epis. Likely staying down here out of the sun is the reason why it was even possible.

I do not have time to marvel at that now. How am I going to defuse this situation? They have reason to be frightened of a strange Zmaj appearing, I suppose. I could crush all of them quite easily, and they do not know I have no intention of hurting any of them.

However, I soon realize I do not have to find a way to appear harmless—which is good. I do not think I could have accomplished such a feat.

Kate steps in front of me, her spine straight, her eyes meeting Annabel's unflinchingly. My own personal heroine. I keep my smile inside, not wanting to belittle her stand even as pride suffuses me. Brave, intelligent, caring. My mate's list of attributes is long indeed.

"You're not afraid of my mate, are you Annabel?" she asks in a clear voice, pitched to carry to all listening.

The shock on all their faces is quite clear, even without the sudden silence that descends. Ah, I understand. Down here, they have not seen such a pairing before, even though it has become a familiar sight to their counterparts in my community and the city.

"Your mate?" Annabel scoffs after she recovers, turning her attention to Kate. "Are you an animal lover now, Kate?"

I raise a brow at the insult, surprised at the ugliness of the jab, but I do not respond. I will allow Kate to steer this meeting how she desires. She knows this group best after all. People say and do things when they are frightened that they are not proud of later. That may not be the case with Annabel, but I will give her the benefit of the doubt for now.

"Is that what you would call Gomul?" Kate counters, her eyes narrowing at Annabel as she gestures to Father. She does not like how Annabel referred to me. Not one bit. It is odd to have her defending me, but it also warms me in a wonderful manner. "If so, it's because of an *animal* like Errol that any of us are still alive. Or do you not realize that?"

The other females shift restlessly behind Annabel as she flushes with embarrassment, her eyes bouncing from Gomul, who I am not sure she noticed before, back to the group she is supposed to be leading.

I can see from this short interaction alone that the self-proclaimed leader is not quite suited to the job she so clearly wants to hold at all costs, including the well-being of those she should be caring for.

As I watch Kate and Annabel face each other, I notice the contrast. The juxtaposition of the two females is quite striking. Kate herself is a true portrait of a heroine with strength and grace, facing the mean-spirited woman with a clear understanding of who she is and what she stands for, even when her positions are difficult.

Something else is also clear now that I see them face to face. Annabel may have had some power over Kate once to hold her here in these tunnels for so long, but no more. That power is glaring in its loss, and Annabel is not likely to regain it.

By the way Annabel's lips thin while she glares at Kate, I can also see that she realizes what she has lost. She does not relinquish that power easily, does not simply accept the loss. It hurts her ego, her feeling of self-worth. So she lashes out.

This time she alters her approach, deciding to argue

about whether the Zmaj are animals is a losing battle. She is correct.

"I told you if you left that you would not be welcome back," she announces instead, her tone strident as she raises it above the mutters of her own group.

"But don't you want to hear what we found out there?" Kate counters, her eyes drifting over the entire group rather than just Annabel. Appealing to everyone. That will not go over well with Annabel, but I am beginning to see that nothing will be acceptable to her. "Why the others aren't with me?"

The humans start to murmur among themselves again, louder this time, their feet scuffing at this provocative question. I also see them scanning Kate, realizing how much healthier she looks than they do. Wondering why.

Annabel jerks her head from Kate to the other females, no doubt seeing what I am observing. She knows she is losing control by the moment, and her response is more anger. Is that the only way she knows how to respond to anything? Some problems aren't solvable through bludgeoning alone. She should have learned that by now.

"You aren't welcome—" she starts again, her voice rising even higher. At this point, she is almost screaming, her face flushing an ugly red. I wince. Luckily, I do not have to listen for long. Her shrill voice is cut off abruptly by another one, a deeper, calmer one, one that strikes at the heart of me in its familiarity.

"Errol?" I look over at the authoritative voice. Father has clearly had enough of this ridiculous standoff. "Come, my son. Let us continue to my tunnel where we may talk."

"What?" Annabel asks sharply as I turn to follow the ghost from my past who stands in front of me, actual flesh and blood. "You can't just let him in here, Gomul! It isn't safe, and it isn't very considerate of you! I don't..."

157

She continues her complaints, but I tune her out as Father begins to speak.

"Do not mind her," Gomul says as she continues to voice her displeasure. "She is not secure in her authority—with good reason, of course. It pushes her to lash out when it is not necessary, an empty attempt to hold on to her perceived power." He pauses, raising a brow as she continues behind us even though we are clearly no longer listening. "It can be...a bit off-putting," he adds, a hint of irritation finally entering his voice.

He does appear to sum up the situation quite well. And there is no way for Annabel to stop either Father or me. So I take his advice and ignore her tirade. There is nothing I could say that would improve matters. Not when Annabel seems to react to every statement with more anger.

However, I do worry for someone else. But when I glance back at Kate, she gives me a subtle nod, reassuring me she can handle the irate woman.

And I trust her to be able to do so.

KATE

J watch as Gomul and Errol leave, both of their backs and shoulders stiff with tension. I really hope they can work things out, for both their sakes. It's so clear how deeply they both care about each other, even if it may not be clear to them. They're going to have to try to bridge that gap they allowed to form between them when they both knew the other was still alive. A rift that is a real shame now that I see them together.

Seeing them fight side by side, I could see exactly how much of a hand Gomul had in forming who Errol is. Their style of fighting, the way they both throw themselves into danger to protect—even if they didn't have more than a passing physical resemblance, it would have been clear they were at least related.

There's something so oddly full circle about it all. That Gomul would be the one to save me, not once, but twice. First when we crashed and were attacked and then again when he urged me to leave, to go find what else is out there. Then that his own son would save me again, both literally and otherwise.

I find myself waking every morning so much happier than I remember ever being, even on the ship. The fact that I am now the reason why they have a second chance...it's truly humbling.

"Don't think this means *you're* welcome here, Kate. Why don't you go on and wait in the rover for your *mate* to get done talking with Gomul? That's as far in as you should ever come from now on."

I turn my attention back at Annabel's sneering voice, sighing internally. The fact that she had to concede defeat with Errol's entrance already bruised her ego. She's bound to be even more difficult now. Not that's it's easy to tell when she's always in some kind of mood. But I have to try. It's not the rest of the group's fault that she's so stubborn and selfish. I need to be able to get through to them, let them know they have more options waiting for them.

"Don't be unreasonable, Annabel—" I start.

"I'm not being *unreasonable!*" she interrupts, spitting the word out like it disgusts her. Like I just used the most heinous insult, never mind the fact that she just called my mate an animal. "I told you when you decided to take the rover—you would not be allowed back if you went against my orders and left! Was I not clear about that?"

I press my lips together in an attempt not to make this worse, throw more vitriol back at her. It's tempting. Very tempting. But Annabel is letting her emotions do the talking here. And I can't let myself do the same. Not if I want to make any kind of headway.

"Don't you at least want to know what we found out there?" I ask again, appealing not only to Annabel, but the rest of the group. "There's so much you don't know about!"

Annabel's eyes flicker and I see a moment of...panic? I frown. Does she not want the others to hear there's more out there? Maybe she knows she'll lose even more people? Why is she holding on so hard to this setup?

"If you just came to try to convince someone else here to do the same idiotic thing you—"

"I think we should let Kate in."

It takes me a moment to realize someone else has jumped in. To defend me, no less. I turn to the sure voice just as everyone else does too, including Annabel, her gaze narrowed in warning. If she was a cartoon, steam would have been pouring out of her ears at this point.

The athletically built brunette does not wilt under the look.

"Information is never a negative," she continues when she has everyone's attention. "We should at least know what's out there. If it's something better, if it's something we need to defend against. Heck, what if this place isn't habitable in the future or we need help? What will we do?"

Those are some sound points. So, of course, Annabel decides not to address them at all.

"Shut up, Maeve. You don't know what you're talking about here. And last I checked, *I* was in charge. Not you."

I can see Maeve clench her jaw in response, her dark eyes snapping fire. Uh oh. That is not a look I would want directed at me. But Annabel doesn't even turn to look at the woman she's shot down in front of everyone. Alienated completely. That is clearly a mistake. Does she think she's broken everyone so completely? I should be a clear example of the fact that she didn't.

"I think we should let Kate in," Maeve repeats, unbowed. "Even if only for selfish reasons."

"Did you not hear me the first time?" Annabel grits out of clenched teeth, finally turning to glare at Maeve. "I said no!"

"I heard you," Maeve responds calmly enough, though her

eyes still smolder. "But what are you going to do if she comes in? Kill her?"

That sends another ripple of unease through the crowd. The shocked reaction allows me to relax slightly. At least they aren't so far gone that they would follow Annabel in murdering someone. So there's that. Man, the bar has gotten low, huh?

"You—" Annabel starts, taking a step towards the other woman.

I don't know what epithet she planned on using, or if she planned to actually get physical with those fists, but Maeve doesn't let her finish. Though it might have been fun to see her wipe the floor with Annabel. Her arms look a lot harder than Annabel's soft ones. Probably because Annabel is happy to dole out work but not so keen on doing it herself.

"I wouldn't push too hard, Annabel," Maeve says softly. "You definitely have no high horse to ride on here."

Annabel pauses, clearly as confused as the rest of us.

"What?" Maeve asks. "Don't you remember? I saw you. Saw what you did when Kate and the others decided to leave."

Ah. I can see where this is going now. And so does Annabel.

"I don't know what you're talking about," Annabel snaps, drawing herself up. Going with denial. What a surprise. "You should keep your mouth shut about matters that you don't understand. That don't concern you."

"Don't understand?" Maeve repeats, raising a brow. "I don't need to have a high level of comprehension for the shit I saw. It's pretty easy to *understand* when someone is up to no good." She steps towards Annabel. "Did you think nobody would see you when you tried to mess with the rover? Tried to force Kate and the others to stay by sabotaging their only safe means of transport?" She cocks her head to the side. "Or did you think that if one of us did...we would never say anything?"

You could hear a pin drop in that silence. And I have to say, it's pretty damn satisfying to see Annabel at such a loss for words. I can also see that this particular reveal is news to a lot of the woman assembled. They're not on board with Annabel's method of trying to keep us here.

After all, none of us would want to feel like actual prisoners, which is exactly what Annabel had tried to do. Unsuccessfully, sure. But what if I hadn't known how to fix the thing? She could have easily accomplished her goal.

Maeve uses Annabel's silence to her advantage, pushing through the group to reach me. I let her take my arm in her hand.

"Come on, Kate. I know I at least want to hear about everything you saw out there."

All right then. Here's my in. I let Maeve pull me along, feeling a surge of hope. Maybe everyone here isn't as under Annabel's thumb as I feared. I sit down in the common area we have set up, watching as the others slowly drift over despite Annabel's continued fuming. What she doesn't understand is that if she's always angry, the anger has less of an impact than it would otherwise.

"Let's start with something fun," Maeve says with a slight smile. "How did you meet Errol?"

I could see how that might be interesting. I certainly didn't think I'd ever have an actual relationship with one of Gomul's race. Probably because Gomul was the only Zmaj I knew before and I saw him as a father figure. Now Errol...I never saw him as a father figure.

"Well," I start, thinking back to when I first saw Errol. And how he gave me instant goosebumps. Maybe I'll just leave that part out. "It wasn't exactly a formal introduction..."

I skim over the beginning of our trip, which went as

expected. When I get to the guster following us, I hear gasps. All of them have too much up close and personal experience with them to hear that and react with anything but real fear. Annabel chimes right in to that opening, her satisfaction clear.

"I told you not to leave, didn't I?" she goads, looking around at the others smugly. "It's dangerous out there. Too dangerous for us to survive on our own."

"But we did survive," I counter, irritated at her happiness at our misfortune. Can't she think of anything beyond how it pertains to her? "We outran all but one, which I then rammed with the rover. Killing it."

She doesn't need to know that I busted the rover in the process and needed to be saved by Errol after all. It would only make her crow louder and I'm already irritated.

"Wow!"

"What happened then?"

"What about the other guster?"

Annabel settles back again, that pinched look on her face at the excited questions. I have the urge to warn her face will freeze like that if she isn't careful, but I stop myself from making the snide remark. Plus it hasn't frozen yet, so...

"The other guster didn't follow. They must have given up after we gained some distance, so we took the time to harvest the meat from the one we killed. It was plenty to replenish our food supply. That was when Errol found us and offered to show us the city."

"So you just traipsed along behind this stranger like idiots?" Annabel cuts in. "Real smart."

When she puts it like that, it does sound pretty stupid. If I say I felt like I could trust him from the beginning, it won't sound any better. I decide to let the truth out after all.

"The rover needed repairs after the incident with the guster, and Errol was confident that we'd find what we needed in the city. He also said there were more of us who survived the crash and many of them were there."

Luckily, that last bit about more survivors diverts attention from the fact the rover needed repairs. A ripple of reaction runs through the women assembled, just as I knew it would. I remember that feeling of excitement at the confirmation that our small group wasn't the only one here on Tajss. It made me feel so much less alone. That feeling alone may have been worth the trip, honestly.

"And you believed him?" Annabel shoots back. "What if he was just luring you back to his lair? Did you think about that?"

Lair?

I tried to imagine Errol in a lair and just couldn't.

"Yeah, we thought he was telling the truth," I retort. "And you know what? He was." I shrug. "I'm glad we took the risk. Because it means we found out that there is a city. And another Tribe living in caves with a farm and even another mining settlement." I lean towards her. "More importantly, we found out that there are more survivors from our ship."

And sure, Rosalind is having problems with that mining settlement, but it still exists, so I decided to include it.

"Oh wow," Maeve breathes, propping her chin on her hands. "Who survived? What's the city like? Have you seen the village?" She stops to take a breath. "Sorry, I just have so many questions!"

I laugh at the rapid-fire stream.

"That's okay—I totally understand. The city is amazing—the Zmaj were actually really technologically advanced at one point, before there was a war that threw them back into the Dark Ages." I look around at the tunnel. "I guess there's always been the suggestion of something more even just looking at these tunnels. But seeing the city really underlines exactly how advanced the Zmaj were."

That provokes another round of questions, though most of them are again from Maeve. Annabel hovers, her arms crossed and face stern as she listens. She doesn't sound too thrilled about the fact we found more survivors. Which is so crazy to me. Maybe she thinks it's just another thing that will chip away at the small dictatorship she's built here.

"...then Errol helped me fix the rover and we went back to the city." I skip the part where Errol and I get together in a different way, for obvious reasons. "After spending a good amount of time around him...I knew I wanted to stay with him." It's a little surprising that it was really that simple. I just knew. "So I went back to his Tribe's home. It's much smaller than the city, but it's also completely adorable. And because there are fewer people, there's a sense of tight-knit community, you know?"

Like there should be here if Annabel wasn't always hanging over everyone like a dark cloud. But I don't say that as I continue. Between recounting everything and fielding questions, time actually passes quickly.

I almost forget that Annabel is glaring at me the entire time, that sour expression on her face. Almost. But I do find myself glancing towards Gomul's tunnel. And hoping everything is going well.

18

ERROL

I feel the pit in my stomach grow as I follow my father to another section of the tunnels. It was smart of him to build his base here. Not only is it cooler because it is underground, it is also easily defensible. It's one of the reasons he was able to keep such a large group safe, even when they are quite separated from him. I'm not surprised at his clever pick of location. Father had often been multiple steps ahead of everyone else.

I feel another pang of loss, a mourning for those years lost between us. Though that grief is premature, is it not? Perhaps after this talk, he will not want to associate with me. That will be a much bigger reason to grieve.

My thoughts are anxious and dark when we finally stop in a tunnel some distance away from the area the females have claimed as their own. Most likely an intentional separation for Father's own peace. He liked to spend time alone even before...everything. I look around, noticing he must have lived here for some time before meeting the humans, judging from the amenities and comforts he has built around himself.

"Please, have a seat," he says, gesturing to a stool.

I nod, lowering myself down to the sturdy piece.

"Would you like something to drink? Some food?" he asks, looking somewhat confused on how to proceed.

I understand. It feels odd to be so formal with my own father.

"No, thank you. Please sit." I do not like him catering to me like this. It feels wrong.

He takes his time following suit, all of his attention focused on me, just as mine is on him.

Silence descends around us for a few moments, a blankness that mirrors what is going on in my own brain. I do not know how to begin, and am happy when Father takes that burden from me.

"Where have you been all this time, my son?" he asks quietly, his eyes searching my face. "What have you been doing?"

I breathe a silent sigh of relief at the question. It is a good idea to ease into this conversation through a safer topic.

"There was a period of...darkness," I admit. "One I do not like to think on too deeply." That is a gentle way to describe the utter depths to which many of us fell after the Devastation.

"There was one for us all," he agrees soberly, soft understanding in his eyes. "I understand the scars from that darkness."

I nod, feeling my stomach roll. Scars. Yes. But that is not the reason why I feel so untethered. I must now speak of the reason why I hesitated to come here. I need to do so, lance it like the festering wound it is. The weight of it is between us. It forces a distance on us, even though we are physically closer than we have been for years upon years.

"I must admit...I was frightened to face you," I confess, cracking open the door to the conversation we must have.

He frowns, looking away. He does not say I should not have been frightened.

"Things did not...end well between us," he says, his gaze far away.

Facing the same memories I am, no doubt.

"On that we can agree," I say. "I...it is one of my biggest regrets. That things ended so badly between us." I take a deep breath as he turns to look at me once more. "That I was not able to fix it before..."

He sighs, shaking his head.

"My son...it hurt my heart to see you seemingly betraying your own race," he says softly, his eyes shining with tears he does not allow to fall.

I feel a knot form in my own throat at the sight, but I must defend myself, must make him see why I did what I did.

"I did not betray our people," I return, gentle but firm. This is my truth. "Even though it might have appeared as though I did. I thought providing epis to the off-worlders would appease them, at least temporarily. Delay the inevitable." I swallow, my mouth dry. "That is the only reason why I gave them what they demanded when others had protested the practice." I think back to the panic, the chaos that gripped us directly before the war that ended everything. "The path we were on was not working. I was willing to try anything to save those I held most dear." I meet Father's eyes on that note, hoping he can see just how much I love him. "I want you to know...my only intention was to give us more time, time I thought we could perhaps use to our advantage. Find a way to circumvent the looming war." I look away, shaking my head. "I do not regret trying to do so, but I regret that I failed you," I murmur. "Failed you terribly."

I cannot look at him as I utter those last words. I cannot.

"You did not fail me, son," he sighs. I look up in surprise as his hand covers my own. "It was a... difficult time. One of confusion and heightened emotion." He shakes his head, sighing again. "I know you did not betray us now, with the luxury of time to cool my anger and hurt. To clarify my assessment." He squeezes my hand, peering deeply into my eyes. "Do you understand? I know you did not betray us."

I tremble at the touch, at the sincerity in his voice.

"I... you were so angry," I whisper. "You did not want to hear my reasoning, what I had to say-- "

"It was as you say. I wish my head had been cooler," he agrees. "Wish I had trusted more in the son I'd helped raise. I am sorry I did not." He takes a deep breath. "I regret the loss of our relationship even more than you, my son. Can you forgive an old warrior his blindness?"

I turn my hand over to squeeze his back, almost disbelieving. A glimmer of hope cracks through the darkness.

"There is nothing to forgive." And I mean it. My heart is open. It always has been. "Looking back...we all did what we thought was best. And in the end...none of it really mattered anyway, did it?"

The Devastation occurred. Our society crumbled. People...so many people...were just...gone. Father sighs, the weight of the world in that one small sound.

"No. It did not," he agrees. "And part of that was deliberate."

I frown at that. Deliberate?

"How? How was it deliberate?" I ask, wondering if I misheard.

"There was foul play at hand that made this result an almost foregone conclusion. Perhaps that was why I was unwilling to listen to your explanations," he admits. "I knew that despite our heartfelt efforts and our hope to avert the worst...we were unlikely to be successful."

Foul play? I frown.

"But...I do not understand," I murmur, shaking my head. "You knew...knew this was inevitable?"

All of this? The destruction of...everything?

He sighs, his eyes turning inward as he looks back.

"I feared it was," he admits. "Though inevitable is a strong word, I could feel events leading here, momentum towards the end building." He shakes his head. "But no matter how probable it seemed, it was not something I could bring myself to accept." He smiles at me, the guilt clear. "It was part of the reason I was so hard on you, so unbending when you came to me."

I frown, my view of the past changing irrevocably at those words. Rebuilding into something different. Father was and is just another Zmaj after all. He can make mistakes, can be affected by his emotions. My view of him...softens.

Our relationship will be different than the one we had before. Different in a way I cannot predict. But perhaps that is for the best.

However, I still have so many questions, so many loose ends that I want answers for. But Father is done with this talk.

"Enough of the past," he says abruptly. "We have not averted the worst...so now...we make the best of what is." His eyes refocus on me. "You do not know how I fill with joy simply at the sight of your face, Errol. Where do you live now? What is your life like?"

I take a deep breath, clearing the way to think of now rather than what feels like a distant past. Almost...another lifetime. Another Errol.

"I live in a community with other Zmaj males and human females. I am a craftsman there and lend my skills to the nearby city resurrected by one of the humans."

"A village and a city?" he murmurs wonderingly. "That is truly more than I could have hoped for." He tilts his head to the side. "You came here with Kate? How did you cross paths with her?"

"Her rover ceased functioning after she hit a guster with it," I explain, grinning at the memory.

Father's eyebrows climb up his forehead.

"That is...an unconventional use for such a vehicle," he remarks, eyes twinkling with humor. "Though I have come to expect the unconventional from her."

I grin at that observation.

"It is true." I swallow, feeling suddenly nervous. How will he react to the news of my mating? He seems truly happy to see me...will this change that? "Kate is certainly unusual. That drew me to her from the beginning." I pause to strengthen my resolve. Kate is mine. Nothing will change that. "Father...I also have something else to tell you."

"You may tell me anything, my son. What is it?"

Concern is seeping into his eyes. I need to tell him. Not continue to build up the suspense, frighten him further.

"I...it is about Kate. She is...my mate."

He stills, his eyes widening. Should I have waited to tell him this? Perhaps this was still too early in our reunion—

"That is wonderful news!" he exclaims, his face lighting up. "You have chosen well, my son! Very well, indeed! I have spent much time with Kate. Why, I see her as a daughter already!" He rises to his feet, clearly excited. "This deserves a celebration! I will arrange a communal dinner for tonight!"

I smile back, happy to see him so happy at the news, and more than a little relieved as well. It feels as though I am light as a feather now, the problems burdening me suddenly gone. But a dinner? After the scene when we arrived?

"That is not necessary, Father—"

"Nonsense," he interrupts. "I want to celebrate news of my son's mating! To the lovely Kate no less!"

There is no deterring him. I find I do not have the heart to be more forceful in my opposition.

So, soon enough, I find myself sitting in a meal circle with Gomul on one side of me and Kate on the other and Annabel and her group arranged around us. It is not the most comfortable dinner. Judging by the way the other females cast furtive glances at my father, it is quite clear Gomul rarely dines with them.

Kate seems to have broken into the group again, the females all listening as she speaks.

"...I also feel a whole heck of a lot better because of this plant they call epis," Kate explains. "It helps you adapt to the environment. I haven't felt better since we were on the ship! It's really amazing."

Nobody questions that as she explains the plant further. She's gained some much-needed weight, her skin is glowing, her eyes clear, her hair shiny. I can see the others note all these signs of improved health even if they do not verbally acknowledge it. The difference between them and Kate is clear to anyone looking.

"A plant?" Maeve asks when Kate pauses. "Where can we get it? If it's so great, I for one would love to try it!"

She has been asking questions all night, intrigued enough to even risk Annabel's ire. She has also been pointedly ignoring the glares sent her way. Some of the others are just as intrigued as she, though they will not voice their interest with the same enthusiasm Maeve does. Not everyone is strong enough to break from a pack such as this.

"Yes, a plant," Kate answers. "But it apparently only grows in caves dug by these giant worm-like monsters. And they don't really take kindly to people rummaging in their homes."

She looks over at me for confirmation, so I nod.

"Yes," I agree. "Zemlja do not make the epis harvest a

simple or easy matter. I would not advise any of you to attempt it."

"Convenient," Annabel mutters under her breath.

I shake my head. That one cannot let a positive word escape her mouth. How she holds on to power here I do not know. The topic turns to Kate's living arrangements next.

"You've decided to live in the smaller community?"

Kate nods, smiling over at me and taking my hand. "Yes. That's where Errol's home is. And I enjoy the smaller, more tight-knit feel of it anyway."

Maeve nods thoughtfully, opening her mouth to say something else, but then hesitating.

Kate notices. "What is it?" she prods. "Now's the time to ask."

"I..." she glances around at the others, taking in the quietly seething Annabel who hasn't said a word so far other than those she's muttered to herself. "I was wondering if I could...come with you?"

A ripple goes through the group at the question, though I am not surprised. Her questions were too specific, too inter-ested not to be leading in this direction. Kate ignores the reaction of the group, giving Maeve an encouraging smile.

"Of course." She looks at the others. "That's an open invi-tation to any and all of you as well." She turns her attention to Annabel. I can see the nerves in her eyes even though her face appears cool and controlled. "In fact, Rosalind did send a message for you, Annabel. She would be happy to welcome you and everyone else in the group to the city. And from there you could decide whether you would rather live in the city or move to the smaller community."

Silence from the assembled group as everyone waits to see how she will react.

"It'll be a cold day in hell before I bow to Rosalind, of all people," she snarls, flatly rejecting the invitation.

Kate sighs, but not as though the answer is unexpected.

"Annabel, whatever happened on the ship doesn't matter here, and now—"

"You have my answer," she interrupts coldly, standing to leave. "Feel free to pass it on."

Hmm. There are obviously some pre-crash tensions between Rosalind and Annabel. It must be a strong disliking for her to react so rudely. It seems Annabel would rather die than take a single command from Rosalind. Ever. Another indicator that she is not mature enough to lead. Personal squabbles have no place in making decisions for a group. Not when the stakes are so high.

When I look over at Kate to see her reaction to the outburst, I can see she is disappointed, but again, not surprised at this turn of events. She seems to always expect the worst of Annabel. And Annabel seems to always deliver on that expectation.

I squeeze Kate's hand, offering what comfort I can. She smiles at me, shaking off the confrontation and turning her attention back to the remaining females.

"Like I was saying, there's a lot to see if..."

And she is back to attempting to lure more of the humans away from here, putting aside her own feelings for the greater good. My admiration for her only grows the more time I spend around her. I doubt that will change. My mate is truly an impressive female.

19

KATE

I take Errol back to my section of the tunnel after dinner is over. The space is the same as I left it. There isn't really a lack of space down here for such a small group, so I'm not surprised by that. Even if it was changed, I'm too relieved that I've managed to deliver Rosalind's message without my head being torn off to really care. Another part of my relief is that Errol's reunion with Gomul went so unbelievably well.

He looks like a weight has been lifted off his shoulders, his step lighter, his face more relaxed.

"Thank you for pushing me to come," Errol murmurs as we settle down on my old pallet. There isn't much room, forcing us to squeeze in tight. Not that I mind.

"I'm glad it went well." I comb my fingers through his hair, settling it back over his shoulder. "So that we can leave here again soon," I add wryly.

He chuckles, his eyes darkening as his hand smooths down my side to close over my butt.

"Perhaps we can make some happier memories here

before we leave," he says, his eyes moving down to my lips. "So you do not only think of it in a negative light."

A languid heat rushes through me. "Sounds like a good plan to me," I say as he moves in to press his lips against mine. This will definitely make me think of this place with less negativity.

He rolls so that I'm on my back under him, reaching down to take off my clothes. He gets up for the briefest of instants, and when he comes back down, he's also fully naked. I moan and he hisses as naked skin meets naked skin. Everywhere. The touch grounds me in a way I really need after all the stress and anxiety of this trip.

I bite down on his shoulder to muffle the sounds I make as he starts to work himself into me, knowing everything echoes down here. Not that they won't already know what we're doing. I have a moment of embarrassment over that thought.

It doesn't stop me.

I wrap my legs around Errol's slim hips, already sweating as he seats himself fully inside me. I don't think I'm ever going to get used to how completely he fills me up inside. Or how mind-numbing and all-encompassing it is when he actually moves.

I gasp, pushing my face into the side of his neck as he thrusts into me, his powerful body making me feel small and delicate. I never thought of myself in that light before Errol, but he's so physically imposing, the comparison is accurate.

I hum as his hand slides between us to seek out my clitoris, pinching it expertly, rubbing it with just the right pressure, while he continues his smooth in and out motions. I cry out, pushing my fist against my mouth to stifle the sound as I arch up against him in my pleasure. He shudders above me, my own orgasm bringing his own. He's learning my body, remembering every detail of my reactions, and putting all that knowledge to use.

He isn't done with one. He pulls out, flips me over, and then I feel another hard erection sliding back into me. I groan, sinking down while I push my hips up to better receive him. He hits me in a completely different spot in this position, and the first go-around already has me primed. I'm moaning with each thrust, his cock hitting...exactly...the right...

I muffle my cry against the pallet this time, my body jerking, only Errol's hands gripping my hips keeping me up as he pounds into me. He's silent as he reaches his own pleasure again, his hips grinding against mine, his hands slightly rougher as they grip my hips.

We're both breathing hard as we sink down onto the pallet with me underneath him. But he quickly changes position so I'm lying on his chest, our size difference too large for me to be on the bottom.

Oh...wow. The afterglow has my eyes at half mast, my body relaxed on top of his. It only lasts a few minutes before my old chums, anxiety and worry, slowly crawl back in.

"What is it?" Errol asks, sliding his hand soothingly up and down my back. "Why are you tense once more? After I worked so hard to relax you."

I chuckle at that, but then I sigh, and it feels like it comes from all the way down in my toes.

"We're only taking one woman with us in the morning," I say. "Leaving Annabel and her loyal followers here. Again."

"Hmm." He doesn't answer right away, choosing his words carefully. 'I understand your desire to take everyone with us, but we cannot force people to help themselves. Only offer the opportunity to do so." His hand slides into my hair. "And I do not think you should worry in any case. They are not alone here. My father is still in residence to ensure their safety. Even if Annabel completely loses all sanity one day."

I snort out a laugh at that last one. The sad thing is, I can almost see it happening.

"Yeah, Gomul is wonderful," I say. "But he is still just one person. And how can he protect people from themselves?" I rise up on my elbows, so I can see his face. "He isn't a miracle worker."

He nods, his arms wrapping around my waist. "We can always come check on them periodically with your wondrous invention."

Wondrous invention? I can't help the giggle that escapes at that description of the rover, shaking my head as I lean down to kiss his smiling mouth. Errol makes me feel like an actual goddess.

I know I'm a good engineer, but I wasn't the best. At least, not in the eyes of the officials in charge of promoting personnel on the ship. They tended to favor those who were more extroverted, more involved in the politics of it all. More competitive with each other as they tried to reach those elevated positions. Something I just wasn't interested in participating in, to be honest. I learned to be happy with where I was.

It gave me extra time to play around, to work on creations I was truly interested in rather than the ones that seemed the most practical on ship. It led to multiple inventions, including the rover. I daresay it's the best invention to date, despite nobody thinking it was a necessary one before the crash.

Times have changed. Understatement of the year, as we used to say. That rover is worth its weight in gold here on Tajss.

"Kate."

Errol seeks out my mouth, kissing me gently before

relaxing back on the pallet once more, his eyes happy. I like knowing I put that look there.

"Hmm?"

"I would like to have a mating ceremony, following the tradition of the old ways," he murmurs.

I smile, feeling warmth suffuse my heart.

"That sounds nice," I agree.

"I'd like to retrieve my father for it," he adds. "Perhaps some of the others will come back with us then."

My smile fades. It's sweet that he's still trying to make me feel better, but I worry that Annabel has too strong a hold on the others, that they've been beaten down too far.

"Maybe," I say, not wanting to bring the mood down. I force my smile back. "Maybe you can tell me a bit about the ceremony."

He smiles back.

"It is an ancient ritual..."

I listen to his soothing voice as I lay back down on his chest. Eventually, it lulls me into a restful sleep despite my worry, images of the lovely ritual playing through my mind.

The next morning, the mood is somber as we prepare to leave. I am glad to be leaving, though I wish it was with the whole group. Errol is right, though. We can't force people to do anything, even if it is in their best interest.

Annabel does not bother seeing us off, though the others do, a few of them hugging Maeve goodbye and wishing her luck. Gomul is there as well, hugging Errol tightly before he pulls me into an equally firm hug.

"I am overjoyed to call you daughter," he says against my hair.

I feel tears prick at my eyes at the warmth in his voice.

"You're the reason I ever met him in the first place," I respond in a low voice. "Who knows how long I would have stayed here if you hadn't given me a push."

He pulls back, smiling at me. "I do not think you would have. Not for long," he says. "I simply accelerated the process a bit."

I chuckle, shaking my head. I don't know if that's true, though it's nice to see he believes it.

"Safe journey," he says, squeezing my shoulder and nodding at Errol. "I will wait for your arrival prior to the mating ceremony."

Goodbyes done, we climb into the rover, with Maeve settling into the back. I don't feel like I'm leaving home this time.

The drive back to the city is just as smooth as the drive out, and with a whole lot less anxiety, which I really appreciate. I've had enough to last me a lifetime.

Once back in the city, we take Maeve to meet Rosalind and get her settled into her own quarters near the other women.

"Maeve! I'm so glad to see you!" Addison cries out, hugging her close. "Oh man, you're going to love it here..." she says, leading her away.

I grin, my worry for Maeve lessening as she's swept away. She glances back at me over her shoulder, waving. I wave back.

Maeve in good hands, Errol and I take a break to eat before we throw ourselves right into planning for the mating ceremony. It feels like a wedding, something I wasn't sure I'd ever have. As Errol pushes to figure out the earliest date possible, I feel love for him filling me up. It feels wonderful to be so wanted. So loved.

"I'm so lucky to be your mate, Errol," I whisper as we head back to our quarters for the night.

His eyes soften, and he pulls me in against his front. "It is I who am lucky," he returns, leaning down to kiss me.

I sigh as I return it, his lips soft against my own. I want

the mating ceremony, but it isn't necessary. We're already joined together, like two halves of a whole separated for too long.

And I've never been happier.

"So who does the ceremony itself?" I ask.

"Traditionally it would be Visidion," Errol says.

"He's the Tribe's Commander?"

Errol nods. "Yes, it is his to do or pass the right of though, to keep with tradition."

"Okay," I agree.

20

KATE

*S*trangely butterflies dance in my stomach. I don't know why I'm nervous but there's no doubt about it that I am. Errol squeezes my hand reassuringly, sensing my distress or being sweet. Either way it helps.

Errol asks after Visidion and we're directed to Rosalind's office. Walking through the City it's so different than the Tribe's home. It lacks the warmth and connection that I feel there. The life breathing through it.

The City is huge and despite a respectable number of people living here they're not even a half a percent of what it was built to house. It gives the entire area an empty, ghost-town feel.

It isn't long before we're walking past the massive fountain and into the building Rosalind has made command central. There's a bustle and hum of life here that the rest of the City lacks. It's welcoming in its own way, pushing aside the empty sensation.

"Do you have an appointment?" a young girl asks, smiling.

"No," I say, looking at Errol.

"I need to see the Commander," Errol says to her. "It is important. Tribe business."

"Of course," the girl says. "I'll let them know you're here."

Wow, here we are crash-landed on a desert wasteland and we're already putting bureaucracy back into play. You'd think, at some point, we'd evolve beyond the need for it. Taking a seat, Errol and I sit and wait.

The butterflies are back, warring with each other from the way my stomach feels. The girl smiles at us occasionally as we sit and wait while others go in and out of the double doors. Shifting in my seat for the umpteen millionth time I look at Errol.

"We should go," I say. "This is a bad idea."

"Patience, love," he advises, taking my hand and interlacing his fingers with mine.

As if on his cue the doors open and Visidion fills them.

"Errol!" he exclaims. "Come!"

Visidion is a big Zmaj, not the biggest but still an impressive figure. He wears an open cloak with a hood that is tossed back. His scales have a soft blue tint to them and his eyes are emerald green. He holds his arms out wide and Errol walks to his embrace.

"Commander," Errol says.

"Come on in, both of you," he says, cheerfully. "Sorry to keep you waiting. There is a lot happening."

We walk into a classic boardroom setting. An ancient, massive table dominates the space with a mix of stools and chairs set around it. Small lights hang in a row down the middle, but they're not lit up now. Floor to ceiling glass windows look out over the City. In front of those windows is a big, wooden desk, behind which sits Rosalind.

"Hello," she says, glancing up from her work. "Please, have a seat."

"Water?" Visidion asks.

"No thank you," I say, my voice catching in my throat. Damn why am I so nervous?

"Thank you, Commander, no," Errol says taking a stool in front of the desk.

Following his lead, I take a seat, but I'm sitting on the edge, too antsy.

"So, what brings you?" Visidion asks, moving to stand behind the desk, one hand resting on Rosalind's shoulder.

Errol clears his throat and rises.

"Commander, I request that you perform the water ceremony for us," he says, tail swishing side-to-side in quick short strokes.

"Really?" Visidion asks, tilting his head to one side focusing his attention on me.

My cheeks warm under his gaze and get hotter when I notice Rosalind's steely eyes on me. Finding my resolve, I rise to my feet.

"Yes," I say, proud that my voice doesn't waver.

Rosalind seems to weigh my words carefully before nodding. Visidion and her exchange a look before either of them speak.

"Good," Visidion says. "Very good!"

He walks around the desk and pulls Errol into an embrace then turns to me with open arms. I accept the hug as gracefully as I can while doing my best to stay upright. Relief flooding through has made my knees weak.

There's a commotion outside the door causing the four of us to turn right as it bursts open, slamming into the wall with a loud bang.

"It's Mei!" a woman with dark hair, a sharp nose, and a strong jaw exclaims breathing heavily.

"Shit," Rosalind swears leaping her desk in a single fluid motion.

Her white space-leathers that she still wears catch the

sunlight streaming through the windows and reflects it in tiny rainbows and sparkles. She moves like a cat, or a goddess. Or a cat goddess. Watching her move is a thing of beauty. I'd never guess her age but I know, from the ship, that she's much older than I am.

She doesn't wait for anyone, running out the door. Visidion is in her wake, not far behind. The woman who burst in leans against the wall, her chest heaving, sweat pouring down her face.

"You might as well come too," she says. "Amara, by the way, let's go."

"What's happening? Isn't Mei pregnant?" I ask.

"Too many questions, run now, ask later," she snaps, turning and running for the stairs.

Errol and I follow if for no other reason I don't know what else to do. Amara is on the stairs, half a flight ahead of us and running fast.

"Damn stairs," she huffs, leaping down the rest of the flight.

Errol grabs me around the waist, spreads his wings and leaps, catching up easily.

"May I?" he asks, landing next to her.

"Yes!" Amara exclaims.

He grabs her around her waist with his free arm then bounds down the stairwell. Fortunately, it's made for Zmaj so it's much bigger than anything we had on the ship. He'd never get away with this if it was designed for humans.

When we reach the base of the stairwell he bursts out into the open foyer and looks. Amara points to the outside and Errol carries us on, kicking the doors open and bursting out on the plaza. He sets us on our own feet.

"This way," Amara says, running.

Ahead, surprisingly distant, I see Rosalind and Visidion.

Damn they run fast! We take off after them, pounding the pavement until we enter another building that's not far away.

Sweat drips into my eyes. Wiping at it, trying to clear my vision, there's a small group of people huddled outside a closed door. A loud groan drifts through, then I hear panting and a soothing voice, but I can't make out the words.

The group, a mix of women and a couple of Zmaj, glance over. Suddenly I feel awkward and out of place. I'm not part of this group, why am I here? Casting my eyes down I struggle with the overwhelming sensation.

Errol takes my hand and squeezes, pulling me forward. Glancing up, the only people I recognize are Rosalind and Visidion. Some of the others look passingly familiar, I think I've seen them around the City, but I don't know them.

"How long since it started?" Rosalind is asking as we approach.

"She's been in labor since last night," a fair-skinned, red-haired woman like me says.

Rosalind purses her lips, nodding. The tension is so thick it's oppressive. Almost hard to breathe.

"I think she was in labor longer than that Inga, she didn't want to bother anyone," an auburn-haired girl says.

Glancing over to her, she's a curvy woman but more than that there's an obvious bulge that can't be mistaken. She's pregnant too.

"It could be Lana," Inga responds, nodding.

I repeat their names in my head, over and over, trying to commit them to memory. A loud scream echoes from the far side of the door followed by a silence that is so absolute I swear no one is breathing. No one moves, I don't even dare to glance to the side. My eyes are glued on that door, waiting for some sign, anything to indicate what's happening.

The soothing voice sounds again, still calm, then there's a

long, low moan. As one those of us outside inhale sharply, making a loud sound as we break past the moment of fear.

"I don't think they can both survive," Amara breathes. "One was hard enough."

"Enough," Rosalind barks. "Don't even think it."

Amara blushes bright red, nodding as she bites her lip. The others gathered look anywhere but at her or each other.

"They have to make it," Rosalind whispers. "All three of them."

My chest tightens and I swear it's suddenly ten degrees warmer in here. Biting my lip, I look around, hoping to understand. The auburn-haired girl, Lana, moves closer, accidentally bumping me with her growing belly.

"Sorry," she says, softly as she puts a hand on my arm. "Are you okay?"

Shaking my head, I smile but it falters. No, I'm not okay but what right do I have to demand any attention here? These people don't know me, they're not my friends or allies. Obviously their friend is on the other side of that door.

"What's…" I can't form the words so I stop and gather my thoughts. Lana keeps her hand on my arm and looks reassuring.

Is having a Zmaj baby always this hard? I hate to admit I've had dreams of Errol and I having a baby, a family, together. Now, fear grips me with a cold hand that won't let go. If it's this bad, how could I?

"It's okay," Lana reassures, patting my arm. "Take your time."

"What's happening? Is it always… this bad?" I glance at the door.

Lana smiles and no one admonishes me for asking the question, which is a relief.

"It's tough," Lana says.

"It's a total bitch," Amara adds.

Lana closes her eyes and shakes her head. "Amara be nice."

"What?" Amara asks, throwing her hands up.

"Ignore her," Lana says, smiling. "Our bodies aren't designed for the Zmaj babies exactly but it's very doable. We're getting better at managing the pregnancies too."

"Oh, well, good," I say, glancing at the door again.

If this is them getting better, how bad was it before?

"Mei's case is special," Lana says, and her words are accented by a loud roar from the far side of the door and a flurry of unseen activity. "She's having twins."

"Twins?" I ask, incredulous.

"Yes," Lana nods. "No one is talking about it because we're not sure they can both survive the birthing."

"Oh," I say, a black pit opening in my stomach.

Errol places an arm around my shoulders, pulling me tight against him.

"But we've got some equipment and we're prepared for this," Lana assures me.

"They will survive," Rosalind says.

It's a statement, no-- an order. It brooks no doubts or counter thoughts.

The door bursts open and a massive Zmaj fills the opening. His face and chest are covered with scars, but a smile goes from ear to ear. Exhilaration rolls from him in an infectious wave.

"They're here!" he exclaims.

The crowd bursts into applause and excitement. People are jumping up and down, cheering, shouting their joy. The men grab the one in the door and lift him up, carrying him in a circle.

The excitement drops to a low boil eventually then two at a time we're being allowed in to meet the new arrivals. When it's time for Errol and me to go in, butterflies dance in my stomach so hard they're tickling my throat.

He squeezes my waist and I grip his hand so tight I'm surprised it isn't hurting him. The first thing I see is the mother, Mei. She's so beautiful, despite or perhaps because of, having just given birth. She has blonde hair that's almost pure white. It's matted to her head and her face is pale, but she looks like an angel who decided to lie on this bed for a short rest.

She smiles as we enter, pushing herself up on her elbows. The scarred male stands next to her and helps her to sit up.

"Hi!" she says, cheerfully. "I'm Mei, so good to meet you."

"Hi," I answer.

Errol and the male exchange pleasantries. Callista steps out from behind the male whose large size had blocked my view of her. In her arms is a blanketed bundle. She goes over to Mei and lies it on her left side then walks behind the male again.

My heart pounds in my chest looking down at the tiny, perfect face. Little scales, too small to be believed, cover its face and there's the hint of two nubs where it's horns will grow. Its cherubic face is so cute my heart could explode. Its little eyes are scrunched close and its nose is wrinkled up as if expressing its disapproval of how bright the world is.

Calista comes up to the bed again and lies another blanketed bundle on her other side. Mei hooks an arm around the babies and coos to them. The Zmaj leans in close, whispering to each of them. It's such a beautiful, private moment a sense of honor mixes with a feeling of not belonging.

"Come, meet the boys," Mei says, nodding.

Errol and I step forward, heart pounding harder in my chest. The smell of them is something I don't have words for. It's clean, beautiful, it's the smell of creation. I've never smelled anything like it before. It's incredible.

"This is Elneese," she says nodding to her right. "This is Ganeese."

"They're perfect," I whisper.

My fingertips tingle with the desire to touch them. Mei smiles and nods.

"Good, traditional names. Congratulations. Two males, a very auspicious day," Errol says to the Zmaj.

"A good day," he agrees, smiling.

"I'm glad you're okay," I say, forcing myself to pay attention to Mei no matter the gravity of the two babies.

"Me too," she laughs. "That was… the hardest damn thing I've ever done."

She looks down at the babies and tears well in her eyes. She kisses each of them on their tiny foreheads.

"But so, so worth it," she says, looking up at her man.

He leans in and kisses her. This moment is so private and intimate that I take Errol's hand and pull us out of the room. Our time here is done. They need time to themselves.

Outside the crowd has disappeared leaving only Rosalind and Visidion waiting for us.

"Beautiful, isn't it?" Visidion smiles.

"I don't have words," I admit, emotions choking my throat close.

"That is our future," Rosalind says, staring at the door, her voice musing. "Together we are stronger."

The Edict rings in my head. How true it is! Turning to Errol I rise onto my toes and he leans in, kissing me. Wrapping my arms around his neck I lie my head on his chest and listen to the steady beating of his hearts.

I've never been happier or surer of what I want from my life. Somehow, I've found it all here.

EPILOGUE

KATE

"Kate, look how well the flowers are doing! We'll have more than enough for your mating ceremony!"

I grin at the excitement in Nora's voice, walking over to the section of the garden where ornamental plants are being cultivated.

"These are gorgeous," I say, crouching down and touching the soft petals. "They'll go beautifully with the meteorite glass."

"Speaking of meteorite glass—we should go pick some more now that it's nearing dinner time," Fallon points out. "Don't want to lose the light."

"You're right," I say, standing with a smile. "I want enough for our clothes to sparkle."

The idea to use it came from the glass that I'd saved from my first time with Errol. When I'd gathered it, I thought it would just be a keepsake, something that I could take out and reminisce about when I was feeling nostalgic.

Then I wondered if it wouldn't be better to incorporate that very real symbol of our relationship, those lovely memories, into the dress I was going to wear. It felt so right. And as soon as I voiced the idea, all my friends were on board.

"That has to be one of the most disgustingly romantic things I've ever heard," Fallon had commented. "It's perfect."

"We just need to gather more meteorite glass. The pieces you have won't be able to cover your entire dress, let alone Errol's clothes if you want to do that as well," Delilah had pointed out.

So, all the women have been helping gather bits and pieces of it when they can.

The support and excitement while preparing for the ceremony has made me feel even more a part of this community. I used to think of it as Errol's home, but now it's our home, our Tribe.

I follow Fallon, Nora and Delilah out near the wall, careful not to stray too far as we pick through the sand for more pieces. The village had a lot of glass, but Errol already used much of it in the protective wall.

That isn't going to be a problem. I had barely come up with the idea before people were already donating glass for the project, even from as far as the city, which really warmed my heart. A couple more runs and I think that will be more than enough.

I pick up a small piece and carefully set it in my bag with the others, marveling at its shining beauty. I smile to myself, shaking my head. A pretty dress won't make or break the ceremony. But I can't deny that I've missed pretty things living as we have in survival mode since the crash. A little extra sparkle will be nice. There's no harm in having my ceremony be as pretty as I can make it.

Still, it's nice to know I would be happy celebrating my mating to Errol even if we were both in rags, and there weren't any decorations at all.

If I have him, I'm happy. Isn't that just amazing?

ERROL

The water ceremony is an ancient practice, one passed down from generation to generation. Father was an official who often oversaw such unions before the Devastation. I believe finding him again is a sign, one that encourages us not to forget our old ways in this new world, this new era on Tajss.

Tradition is important. It is a part of us, a part of our ancestors that came before. So much of this has been left behind as we devolved into the darkness that came after the Devastation. The bijass claimed our past, our traditions. Traditions imply a hope for the future and we had none.

I, for one, know well what it is to run from your past. I had embraced the bijass, not wanting to face what had come before. You cannot face the future though without freeing your attention from what you have done.

Kate gives me that. She is my desire for the future, for what is to come. I want to commit to her publicly, surrounded by friends and Tribe mates.

"I could have done this for you," Gomul grouses.

"Yes, Father," I agree. "That would be breaking tradition though. We need to be accepted by the Tribe, that means the Commander should be the one to do the ceremony."

"I've done more of these then he ever thought of," Gomul sighs. "But you are right son. I'm proud of the man you have become."

My scales itch at the compliment, warming to his words. Meeting his eyes, I don't have words, so I simply pull him into an embrace.

"I am glad to have found you," I say.

"And I you," he says, patting my back.

"Am I ready?" I ask, holding my arms out to either side.

He looks me up and down with a critical eye before nodding. Smiling, I place an arm around his shoulders and we walk out to the ceremony.

The other males are gathered wearing the traditional robes and standing in a line facing each other. They hum as I walk between them, my father at my side. Visidion stands at the end of the line. My father takes his place next to Visidion.

Turning to face the cliff, I wait. My hearts beat a slow, steady rhythm in my chest, pounding but not too hard. Then Kate walks out of the cave where she was preparing with the other females. My hearts stop. Breath catches in my throat. The world goes still. Even the wind doesn't dare blow for fear of touching the beauty that is my mate.

Kate sparkles, literally, her dress reflects sunlight in a dazzling display. It accents the pure perfection of her face in ways that I cannot even begin to take in with one look. My hearts pound, hard, trying to break free of my chest and fly across the distance between us to her. I am hers, her claim is deep and true.

She stands at the top of the ramp leading down to the floor of the Tribe's home and smiles. The suns do not compare. The other females pick up the train of her dress and help her down. As she walks with them towards me, I'm light-headed.

The males form a tunnel with their lochabers, arms extended up, blades at the middle of the space between them. Kate walks down the tunnel, her eyes locked on me. I see, from here, the moisture twinkling in the corners of her eyes but the smile on her face tells me they are from joy.

When she steps out of the tunnel formed by the males, I take her hands and guide her so that we stand facing each other in front of Visidion and my father. I can't take my eyes off her. Nothing in the universe could be more beautiful than she is right now.

The Commander lays his hands on ours, gripping them. His cool hands are almost cold, despite the heat.

"Errol," he says, his voice deep and commanding. "Your heart has yearned and has been answered. Is this the female you would share water with?"

"It is," I answer.

"Kate, your heart has answered the call. Is this the male you would share water with?"

"It is," she answers, no hesitation.

The Commander holds his hands on ours a moment longer then steps back. Drosdan and Padraig walk forward, carrying a massive barrel between them.

They set the barrel down with a grunt between Visidion and us. The Commander comes back, motioning my father to join him. He takes the lid off the barrel. Inside is water, cold, cool, refreshing water. An excessive amount. The Commander nods to my father, who's eyes open wider then he nods.

"Water brings life," my father says, taking over the ceremony. "In sharing water, you commit one to another and both to all of us. Our future rests on you."

He places his cupped hands in the barrel then pours water over my head. Stepping back to the barrel he gets another handful of water then pours it over Kate's head. She gasps as the cold liquid drips down her face, spluttering. He steps back and I step to the barrel, cup my hands and draw water, turning to Kate.

"I give you my water," I say, pouring water over her head.

"I take your water," she answers.

She smiles broadly then steps to the barrel. She cups her hands in it then glances at me, arching an eyebrow. Smiling I lower myself to my knees. There's a round of laughter from the females where they watch but the males don't react.

Kate takes her hands out and pours the water over my head.

"I give you my water," she says.

"I take your water," I say.

Cheers surround us with warmth and love as I leap to my feet and swing her up into my arms. Locking my lips to hers, I kiss her with every ounce of passion that exists in the universe. She is my treasure.

Breaking the kiss at last, I set Kate back on her feet, keeping my arm around her waist, we turn to face our Tribe, our home, and they rush forward to welcome us.

THE END

ABOUT THE AUTHOR

USA Today Bestselling Author of fantasy and scifi romance, Miranda Martin's books feature larger than life heroes with out-of-this-world anatomy and smart heroines destined to save the world. As a little girl she would sneak off with her nose in a book, dreaming of magical realms. Today she brings those fantasies to life and adores every fan who chooses to live in them for a while.

She was born and raised in southern Virginia, but as a veteran she's traveled to places like Korea, Hawaii and good 'ole Texas. Now she's settled in Kansas, the heart of America, with her husband and daughters. Her favorite animals are dragons, unicorns and cats. If she's not writing, you can still find her tucked away somewhere with a warm blanket and her nose in a book.

Get in touch!
mirandamartinromance.com
miranda@mirandamartinromance.com

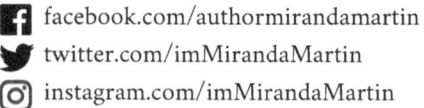

facebook.com/authormirandamartin
twitter.com/imMirandaMartin
instagram.com/imMirandaMartin

ALSO BY MIRANDA MARTIN

USA TODAY BESTSELLING AUTHOR

Red Planet Dragon's of Tajss Series
Red Planet Jungle Series
The Power of Twelve Series
The Alva Series
Dragon's & Phoenixes Series